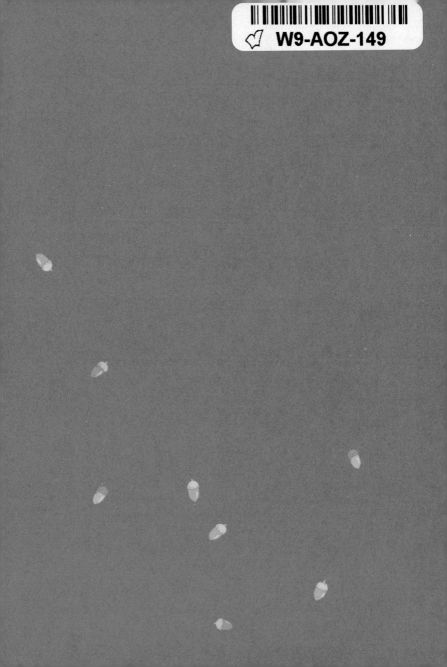

# My Neighbor TOTORO

**Art and Story by**
**Hayao Miyazaki**

**Text by**
**Tsugiko Kubo**

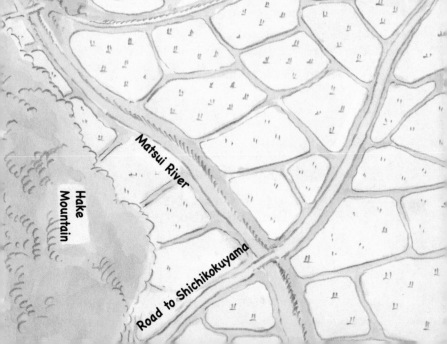

**Highway**
(This isn't a high speed highway. Just a state road.)

**Shrine**
(Oinarisama, shrine to foxes often erected near farm fields.)

**Matsugo Village**

**Kanta's home**

Matsui River

Hake Mountain

Road to Shichikokuyama

Tea Field

Azuma Railroad Line

Vegetable
Field

Forest

Big camphor tree

Satsuki and
Mei's home

Shin Pond

Rice paddles

The road to Satsuki and
Kanta's school

Village where
Satsuki and
Mei live

# Map of Matsugo
Circa 1955

**My Neighbor Totoro**

"Shosetsu Tonari no Totoro" (My Neighbor Totoro: The Novel)
Original story and illustrations by Hayao Miyazaki
Written by Tsugiko Kubo
Copyright © 1988 Studio Ghibli
© 1988 Tsugiko Kubo
All rights reserved.
First published in Japan by Tokuma Shoten Co., Ltd.

English translation © 2013 VIZ Media, LLC
Design by Yukiko Whitley

Published by VIZ Media, LLC
P.O. Box 77010
San Francisco, CA 94107

Library of Congress Cataloging-in-Publication Data

Kubo, Tsugiko, adapter.
    My neighbor Totoro : a novel / art and story by Hayao
Miyazaki ; text by Tsugiko Kubo ; translated by Jim Hubbert.
        pages cm
    Summary: "Eleven-year-old Satsuki and her sassy little
sister Mei have moved to the country to be closer to their
ailing mother. While their father is working, the girls explore
their sprawling old house and the forest and fields that
surround it. Soon, Satsuki and Mei discover Totoro, a magical
forest spirit who takes them on fantastic adventures through
the trees and the clouds—and teaches them a lesson about
trusting one another"—Provided by publisher.
    ISBN 978-1-4215-6120-2 (hardback)
    I. Hubbert, Jim, translator. II. Miyazaki, Hayao, 1941–
Tonari no Totoro. English. III. Title.
    PZ7.K948533My  2013
    [Fic]--dc23
                                            2013023521


Printed in the U.S.A.

First printing, October 2013
Ninth printing, June 2021

# My Neighbor Totoro

Original Story and Art by Hayao Miyazaki
Novel by Tsugiko Kubo
Translated by Jim Hubbert

STUDIO
GHIBLI
LIBRARY

# My Neighbor TOTORO

1. The New Old House     9

2. Is the House Haunted?     38

3. Mother     59

4. Mei Meets Totoro     82

5. The Rainy Day     105

6. The Bus Stop at Inari Shrine     133

7. Totoro's Gift     158

8. Summer Vacation     177

9. Mei Goes Missing     200

10. Thank You, Totoro     227

## 1. The New Old House

The little three-wheeled truck rolled along the country road.

"May and May, riding along in May," Tatsuo sang cheerfully. His white cap was pushed back on his head. "On the way to Happy-Go-Lucky Forest…"

Uncle Fujiyama was planted next to him in the driver's seat. He gripped the steering wheel with both hands, stared straight ahead, and chimed in, "Onward!"

Satsuki leaned out from the flatbed behind the cab. Her face was shining. "Daddy, here's some caramel for you and Uncle." She gave him two pieces of caramel wrapped in paper.

"Oh-ho, that's very thoughtful."

The three-wheeler putted merrily along in the sunshine under the blue dome of the sky, past fields of wheat like an ocean of green that stretched as far as the eye could see.

*Putt-putt. Rattle-bang. Bump-squeak putt-putt.* The truck was jolting and swaying so much, Satsuki was afraid her caramel would leap out of her mouth.

"Uncle Fu-Fu-Fujiyama…"

"How're you doing back there?" he yelled over the noise of the engine.

"How, how f-far…S-sorry, everything's sh-shaky."

"That's a country road for you."

"Ho-how much f-farther is it?"

Tatsuo laughed. "Better hold on, unless you want to fall out."

"I'm f-fine!"

"About fifteen minutes to the bus stop by the house," said Uncle.

Tatsuo wiped the dust off his spectacles with the tail of his shirt. "That means we should be there in about twenty minutes."

"Yaaaay!" Satsuki cheered. She ducked down under the writing desk where her little sister Mei was sitting on the floor of the truck. Tatsuo and Uncle started singing again.

"May and May…"

"Onward!"

Tatsuo and Uncle Fujiyama were archaeologists

who had been close friends since high school. They invited each other on digs and even wrote reports together. Whenever the family of one needed help, the other would pitch in.

Yasuko, Satsuki and Mei's mother, had contracted tuberculosis a year ago. Now she was at the sanatorium at Shichikokuyama Hospital. When the time came for her to go, Uncle Fujiyama took her there himself.

Now the rest of the family was moving to a new house. Things were going to be better, and Satsuki was very happy.

The doctor said that soon Yasuko could leave the sanatorium and get better at home. So they were moving to Matsugo, a village that was much closer to the hospital.

Satsuki was so happy she was fit to burst. And as always, Uncle Fujiyama came along to lend a hand. He wasn't a very good singer, though. All he could say was "Onward!" He was famous for his terrible singing.

Saturday morning, in the month of May. Summer was just around the corner.

The sky was so blue. And so big!

The road was lumpy and bumpy, and it kept going on and on!

The breeze caressed the wheat, and the sun flashed off the rippling stalks, gold and green. The three-wheeler, piled high with all their furniture, banged and bumped along the road as the wind blew playfully.

"May and May…"

"Onward!"

In Japanese, *Satsuki* was the old name for the month of May.

"Riding along…"

"Onward!"

Mei was four years old. Her father had named her after the month of May too. May and May were moving to a new home in May.

"We're on our way to Happy-Go-Lucky Forest…"

"Onward!" cried Mei, as she worked to peel the wrapper off a piece of caramel. Mei was very small. The leg well under Tatsuo's writing desk was more than big enough for her to hide in. It didn't matter whether the three-wheeler jumped up and down or side to side, she was just fine. Satsuki had carefully piled pillows and cushions around her. This made things even more comfortable.

"I'll do it for you, Mei. Give me the caramel," Satsuki said.

"I'm okay."

"You can't unwrap it yourself."

"I'm okay."

"It's too shaky back here."

"I'm okay," Mei said. "Everything is oooohkay." She put the caramel in her mouth with the paper still stuck to it and chewed it.

"I bet that tastes awful," Satsuki said.

"I'm okay. It tastes good."

Little Mei was quite thin. One would almost have thought she wasn't getting enough to eat. Her fine hair was gathered in pigtails to either side and stuck out behind her ears, making her look like she was all head. Her eyes were serious and smaller than her sister's. Her nose was round and her baby teeth were gappy, not like Satsuki's straight white teeth. But in a mysterious way, she looked adorable. When she smiled, her cheeks dimpled and her dark, shining eyes looked at you steadily.

"I could've got that paper off for you, Mei."

"Everything is okey-dokey."

Two sisters, Satsuki and Mei. Their mother had been in the hospital for a whole year. Satsuki was seven years older than Mei. She loved to read, and she could run faster than anyone in school. Everybody agreed that when it came to a fight,

Satsuki Kusakabe could hold her own against any kid in the neighborhood.

"I can take the paper off the cama-mel myself. I'm a big girl now." Though she was only four, Mei was determined to be just as independent as her big sister.

"Oh no!" Satsuki yelled. "Hide, Mei. Keep your head down!"

A startled Mei shrank back under the desk. "What happened? What's wrong?"

"A policeman."

"Police!" Mei squeezed her eyes shut.

*Putt-putt, bang, putt-putt.*

"Satsuki!" Mei whispered. She couldn't bear the suspense.

"Shhh!"

"If he catches us, will we go to the jail?"

"Be *quiet*!"

*Putt-putt, pop-putt pop-pop.*

The three-wheeler kept burbling its lazy song without slowing down at all. "Please, God," Mei whispered. "Please, Daddy. Please, Mommy. Satsuki. Help me. Don't let them put me in the jail."

Satsuki laughed. "Oh, this is silly. I worked my-self up there for a second." She leaned out of the truck and started waving. Now it was Mei's turn to scold.

"Satsuki, hide!"

"Look, Mei. It's just the postman."

The postman riding slowly along on his bicycle waved as they passed. Satsuki and Mei looked at each other and laughed. They dove under the desk and tumbled about in the pillows and cushions, laughing and giggling.

Mei leaned out the side of the truck. "Look, a cemetery!"

"Where? Oh Mei, look at that. A big crow!"

All of a sudden, Mei looked very serious again. "Satsuki, if there's police …" She gulped nervously. "Do we have to go to the jail?"

"I don't know. We'd have to pay some money, probably."

The pile of furniture and household things in the back of the truck would be enough to get them fined. That's what Aunt Kyoko had said to Tatsuo before they left. Anyone could see the three-wheeler was overloaded.

"It'll get the job done," Tatsuo had said with a laugh. He told Aunt Kyoko this would save them money moving all their things. The big chest of drawers. All the bedding and Tatsuo's writing desk and chair. The kitchen cupboard and their round dining table. The bicycle, a big bench, the pots and the kettle, the rice bin, their umbrellas, and the washbasin for washing dishes and the washboard for washing clothes. And hundreds of books and boxes of reports and papers and Tatsuo's archaeological tools. He had taken the broken old clay pots and pieces of rock that he had dug up and stored most of them at the university. But everything else was piled in the back of the truck. And the two little girls were to ride in the back as well, though that wasn't allowed.

"I think we'll be fine." Early that morning, as they carried their things out of the big Terashima house and loaded them onto the cargo bed of the blue three-wheeler, Tatsuo and Uncle Fujiyama kept surveying their work and repeating, "I think we'll be fine."

The little three-wheeler was a sight to behold. As the two friends tied down the mountain of furniture with rope, Grandmother Terashima had clapped her hands and said, "It looks like a big pomegranate that burst."

Yasuko had grown up in the rambling old Terashima house near the heart of Tokyo, with the huge cherry tree rising above the black clapboard fence. Satsuki and Mei lived with their parents on the second floor—ten years for Satsuki, four for Mei. Now they were headed for Matsugo. No longer would they be surrounded by relatives.

Satsuki and Mei were eager to be off and thrilled to ride in the back of the truck. "I think you'll be fine," Uncle Fujiyama said. "Hop aboard. There's no room up front."

"They'll be fine," said Tatsuo.

Aunt Kyoko had always had a sharp tongue, but today was worse than usual because she was worried.

"I can't believe you're letting them ride back there!" she snapped at Tatsuo. "If the police see you, they'll haul you in and give you a fine. Now listen, you two"—she turned to Mei and Satsuki—"don't hang out the side gawking. If you want to stay out of jail, keep out of sight, you hear?"

Satsuki was on pins and needles that Aunt Kyoko would insist they take the train. As she and Mei climbed into the truck and under the desk, her heart was pounding.

But she had nothing to fear. Tatsuo taught at the university and wrote long reports "full of words," as Satsuki put it. But compared to Aunt Kyoko, he was very quiet. "They'll be fine," he said again. And with another "They'll be fine" from Uncle Fujiyama, the truck pulled out of the yard with Satsuki and Mei ensconced in the back.

*Rattle-bang, putt-putt, putt-putter-putter.*

When Yasuko had first gotten sick, Aunt Kyoko had told their father, "If you were a little more careful, your wife wouldn't be in the hospital now."

*That is* so *stupid*, thought Satsuki, who had overheard. *Daddy loves us and cares about us. Mommy got TB because she got the TB bug, that's all. It wasn't Daddy's fault. I don't like you, Aunt Kyoko. So there!*

Satsuki looked back down the road. Her aunt was somewhere under that endless blue sky. She stuck her tongue out as far as she could. Then she threw back her head and laughed.

"Ha ha! Big trees! Beautiful, beautiful, beautiful trees!"

How that three-wheeler shimmied and shook! Everything they could see from the back of the truck seemed shiny and new. No matter if it was beautiful or dirty, interesting or boring, it was all fascinating.

"Look, Satsuki, there's a little shop," Mei said.

"I saw it. It was falling apart."

"You said it!"

The three-wheeler threw up clouds of dust as it rolled down a road lined with plum trees. It passed a bus stopped in front of a rustic little general store. There was a wooden signboard hanging from the eaves that said TSURUYA.

*Putter putt-putter.*

Tatsuo reached back and banged twice on the side of the truck. "That's the bus stop," he called out. "We're almost there."

"Inari Shrine? Is that the name of the stop?" Satsuki shouted back. She wasn't sure if she was reading the characters for *Inari* correctly.

"That's right, Inari Shrine. There's a pretty little shrine just up the road here."

But it hardly looked pretty to Satsuki. The crimson paint was peeling off the gate. The shrine was stained black and brown from long years of exposure to the elements. Dusty cobwebs that looked hundreds of years old hung everywhere.

The three-wheeler tilted as it turned sharply onto the little road just past the shrine. Satsuki and Mei were anxious to find out what the house looked like. The truck bounded up and down over the uneven road. It bored through a dark grove of trees like a tunnel, then out into the sunlight again, with farmland and shining rice paddies spread out before them.

"Okay, you two. We're here," shouted Tatsuo. "This is Matsugo. Beautiful, don't you think?"

"Yes!" Satsuki said.

"Yes!" Mei said, just like Satsuki.

After that the sisters were quiet for a long time. They leaned out and looked over the fields and forest with eyes that were surprised and a little shy.

Beneath a scattering of shining white clouds, in a sky so blue it was almost purple, a line of birds, calling into the distance, crossed overhead.

A pear orchard in full flower swayed gently in the wind, like a white cloud hugging the earth. Small stands of trees were scattered along the borders between the rice paddies. Grass-covered footpaths ran between them on low dikes, with dandelion flowers winking up out of the grass as if they were tiny yellow suns. The wind whispered softly through the fresh, sparkling air. Now and then the lowing of a cow floated to them on the breeze. The three-wheeler putted along, more slowly now.

Tatsuo had asked if they thought it was beautiful. But for Satsuki and Mei, everything was so new and different, they weren't sure what to say.

"I don't see anybody," Mei said.

"Look there." Satsuki pointed to a group of farmers at work in a paddy. "See? And there's a horse too."

"There's no *little* people," Mei said.

"You're right. I don't see a single one."

Satsuki told herself she would have to see the school and their new house and a lot of other things before she decided whether or not this was really a good place to live. "I don't see a single one," Satsuki said again after a pause.

"Maybe they went to school," Mei said uncertainly.

"Yep, that must be where they all went."

So it was a surprise when the three-wheeler suddenly stopped alongside a boy loading hay into a wheelbarrow on an embankment overlooking the road. The boy looked to be about Satsuki's age. Afterward, Tatsuo told her that his name was Kanta Ogaki. He was the grandson of the old lady who was taking care of the house Tatsuo had rented.

After Tatsuo had finished paying his respects to the Ogaki family, they started off again. The three-wheeler turned down a gravel road that was easier going than the dirt road they had just left.

"Daddy?"

"Yes, Satsuki."

"Are we almost there?"

"Almost."

"How many minutes?"

"Should be two or three."

Satsuki turned and saw the little boy getting smaller. He was still watching them from the embankment.

"Daddy?" Satsuki leaned out of the back toward the cab.

"What's up?"

"That boy looked kind of like a fourth-grader."

"Could be."

"If he's a fourth-grader, he'll be in my class."

"I guess he will."

"He didn't say hello or anything," Satsuki said.

"He's probably too shy."

"Really? But how come he's not in school? It's Saturday."

Uncle Fujiyama kept looking straight ahead as he yelled back, "Planting break."

"A school vacation to plant the fields?" Satsuki was surprised.

"Just for a few days. Lucky, aren't you?" said

Tatsuo, laughing. "All right," he shouted happily. "We're home!" Uncle stopped the truck and they all got out.

A little bridge of stone over a brook that ran along the side of the road led to a stone gate and a narrow path that sloped steeply up through the trees.

"Is this our stream?" Satsuki said.

"You could say that," Tatsuo said.

Satsuki was astonished. "Even the fish?"

"Come on, Mei!" Satsuki raced across the bridge and up the path. The trees on either side made a beautiful green ceiling of branches. Tatsuo had told her she'd find the house when she got to the top.

And he was right. But as it floated into sight, the house almost seemed to shrink back a little sadly, as if embarrassed to be seen.

The house was surrounded by the bushy new weeds of early summer. It looked as if it were about to start listing, like a forlorn sailing vessel that had seen too many storms.

"It's falling apart!" Mei exclaimed. She had followed Satsuki right up the path.

"It sure is," Satsuki almost shouted with surprise. In fact it looked like a haunted house.

"Really, really falling apart," Mei said.

"It's not only falling apart, it's falling apart beyond falling apart!" Satsuki said.

The two girls broke into happy laughter. "Falling apart! Falling apart!" Their voices seemed to bounce off the house in a happy echo. They suddenly felt very hopeful that everything would turn out well.

"I like it!" shouted Satsuki.

"I like it too!" yelled Mei.

Falling apart. The house was once painted brown, but the paint had weathered to gray. The red tin roof was mottled with rust. The more they looked at it, the more the house seemed about to collapse. The storm shutters probably hadn't been opened for ages. The windows were coated with dust. And the closer they got, the more tattered and old the house looked.

They walked around to the south side and found an old wisteria trellis. The uprights and the lattice overhead were so rotted and eaten away by insects that it looked like it might collapse any moment. Satsuki gave one of the uprights a playful shove. The trellis swayed, and a torrent of white paint flakes fell from the lattice.

"Ugh, it's raining paint!"

/

"Satsuki, this is really loose. Maybe it's going to fall down?" Mei was always eager to imitate her big sister. She gave the post a shove. She pushed so hard her face turned red. Pieces of the trellis started falling off.

The sisters roared with laughter and ran off toward the garden. There was lots more to see and explore.

The garden was a surprise too. Perhaps it was because it had been left untended for so many years, but it was unlike any garden they'd ever seen. They could hear frogs chirping in the grass. A corner of the garden held the remains of a little pond, a weedy depression bordered by a ring of large stones. The wind swayed the purple irises growing among the weeds and zinnias so crimson that they looked almost poisonous. Gossamer butterflies rose up in little swarms and fluttered away.

"I bet spooks come here to play," said Satsuki, and she did a somersault in the grass. Then she looked up and saw it. "Mei, just look at that tree!"

The woods ran along the east side of the yard. The light was dim among the tall, thick trunks, but above them all rose another, darker tree, spreading its enormous branches over the forest and toward the sky. The branches swayed slowly in the wind, like the wings of a giant bird. It was more a creature than a tree.

"Have you ever seen anything so *big*?" Satsuki said.

"Ahhh," Mei couldn't hold it back. "Choo!" She had been looking up at the blue, blue sky with her mouth open for so long that she had to sneeze. The girls were still staring up at the tree with wonder when they heard the storm shutters rattle. Tatsuo was opening them one by one.

"Look, Daddy! This tree is so big, it's unreal!"

"Mm-hm. That's the Tsukamori laurel. Pretty impressive, isn't it?"

"Tsukamori?"

"That's the name of the woods," Tatsuo said.

"It's a laurel tree?" Satsuki said.

"Yep. A camphor laurel."

"It's really huge, Daddy."

"I think it must be a hundred feet tall."

"It looks like some kind of monster," Mei said.

"It's been here for hundreds of years, so it *is* a monster, in a way."

"Cam-fer lor-rel. Cam-fer lor-rel," said Mei, trying it out. Satsuki turned toward the tree, bowed deeply, and put her palms together.

"Hello, Mr. Camphor Laurel. My name is Satsuki Kusakabe. We just moved here. I'm in the fourth grade. I hope we can be friends."

They ran toward the house. Tatsuo had opened the sliding glass doors that looked out on the garden. The floor of the house was almost two feet higher than the ground outside. They leaned in and peered inside for the first time. With each shutter Tatsuo opened, more light came in. The house smelled moldy.

Beyond the wood-floored corridor that ran just inside the sliding doors was a tatami room with an alcove in the far wall. Something on the floor caught Satsuki's eye. "Hey!"

"What is it?" Mei said.

"I don't know. I saw something shining." Satsuki stepped up into the house.

"What are you doing? Take your shoes off!" said Tatsuo.

"But…it's just…I'll be right back." Satsuki was so distracted by what she'd seen that she couldn't give a straight answer. She was so eager to find out what it was that instead of slipping off her sandals, she walked across the floor on her knees, feet in the air behind her.

"Got it!"

"What did you got?" Mei squinted into the gloom.

"An acorn. Here's another one!" Satsuki found a second acorn not far from the first. Both of them were round, green, and shiny.

"What have you got there?" Tatsuo came over to take a look. He shook his head, puzzled. "A green acorn in May? That's odd. At this time of year, it should be brown." He was about to say more when Uncle Fujiyama shouted from the yard.

"Hey, Kusakabe! Where do you want this?" He was unloading a heavy old gramophone from the truck.

"We'll put it in the corridor for now." He went out to help Uncle Fujiyama.

Mei tugged at Satsuki's skirt. "What?" said Satsuki, looking down. Mei held a slender little hand toward Satsuki.

"I got one too."

"Satsuki!" Tatsuo returned and handed her a key. "Take this and open the back door to the kitchen."

"Okay."

"I'm going too!" Mei said. They jumped down into the yard. As they walked around the house toward the back, Mei said proudly, "This fell right on my head." Her acorn was shiny and green, just like Satsuki's.

"You mean from the ceiling?"

"Mm-hm."

"That's crazy. There's not supposed to be anybody here."

"The ceiling threw it at me."

"Are you sure it wasn't Daddy?"

"No. He was out in the garden."

The sisters walked in the sunshine through the tall, soft grass to the back of the house.

Where had the acorns come from? Were they a gift from someone? Tatsuo had seemed surprised that they weren't brown. Satsuki opened her hand and looked at the acorn again. Was there something in the house? *Mice, or maybe squirrels?*

*Ghosts?* No way.

But Satsuki *had* felt something watching them from the moment she first saw the house. It was as if something vigilant were observing them carefully.

Maybe the walls of the house were watching them silently. Or was it the giant tree? Or the wild mint? Or the plume grass, or the clover? Looking at them, watching them?

Satsuki giggled. "Anyone in there?" She rapped the side of the house.

The house didn't answer.

Well, of course it didn't.

The sun stared down from the empty sky and wrapped them in light. Somewhere nearby they could hear the rumble of a passing train.

Mei took Satsuki's hand. Satsuki was surprised. This wasn't like Mei.

"What if there's ghosts?"

Satsuki thought Mei might be scared, but when she looked down, she saw a curious smile instead. She stuck the key in the back door, turned it in the lock, and looked at Mei. "In that case, we'll just have to ask them what they're up to."

But after that, everything happened so fast that there was no time to ask any questions at all.

The moment the door swung inward, the kitchen came alive with a whirring and a scurrying and a scuttling. Little balls of fluff darker than charcoal were swarming all over the floors and walls and ceiling!

Perhaps because the darkness in the house was so sudden after the light outside, Satsuki wasn't sure whether to trust her eyes. The whole room seemed to heave and writhe in front of her. Yet the next moment, there just was a shabby gray kitchen, like one you might see in any old house. Satsuki gasped with astonishment.

Whatever she had seen—a cloud of dust, a swarm of insects, *something*—had fled instantly. Now the kitchen not only looked bare, it looked as though it had been scrubbed clean.

Satsuki stood gaping at the empty kitchen, then turned to look at Mei.

Mei's eyes were bulging so much she couldn't blink. She must have seen them—those swarming, writhing, scurrying black somethings—as well.

Mei's nostrils were open as wide as her eyes. Satsuki took one look and started to laugh. She gave Mei's nose a squeeze. "What do you think you're doing?"

"Spooks." She pushed Satsuki's hand away. "This house has spooks!"

"Are you sure? Maybe it's just bugs or something."

"No. That was spooks." Mei looked up at her sister. "It is okay to catch 'em?"

"Why not? They're ours." Satsuki thought this might be a good idea. It would be hard to relax until they found out what they had seen. Okay, then!

"All right Mei, I'll catch one for you. We'll scare

them out by yelling as loud as we can. Ready?"

The two girls burst into the kitchen, yelling at the top of their lungs, throwing open every cupboard and drawer. They even went into the bath next to the kitchen and pulled the cover off the old iron bathtub to see if there was anything inside.

They didn't find a thing. Not one single something.

It was as if the fluff balls had been a dream. The little changing area next to the bath was dark and empty too.

"That's very odd," Satsuki said. Where had they all gone to? Maybe their eyes were just playing tricks on them?

"Come out, Mr. Spooks. Come out." Mei was still searching intently. "Please? Just one of you is okay. Please come out."


"Soot sprites. That's what those are."

Satsuki and Mei were telling their father what had happened when they heard a voice from the living room.

"Soot sprites?" Satsuki answered without knowing who it was.

"First thing they do is run away, faster than you can blink," said the voice. "Am I right?"

"That's Mrs. Ogaki," Tatsuo told the girls. "She's looking after the property."

Satsuki went to introduce herself and found a tiny, kindly looking old woman busily dusting the room. To Satsuki, she looked as if she had always had her white hair and deeply lined face.

"Hello. My name is Satsuki. Satsuki Kusakabe."

"Pleased to meet you. You can call me Granny." The woman took the cloth she had wrapped around her hair to keep off the dust and slowly folded it with rough red hands. "So these are your daughters, Professor? What adorable little girls."

Satsuki immediately felt drawn to this tranquil old woman.

"Don't you pay those soot sprites the least little mind, now," said Granny Ogaki. "They won't do any harm." She turned to Tatsuo. "I hope you forgive me. I wanted to have the place dusted and aired out before you got here, and I would have too, if my rheumatism wasn't bothering me so. Soot sprites! This old house must be on its last legs. I hope you won't think it's haunted."

"Not at all. To be honest, it's cleaner than I expected. We'll be just fine." Tatsuo didn't seem interested in learning more about soot sprites. He put the sideboard down in the living room and hurried off to the three-wheeler for more furniture.

Granny went into the kitchen, pumped some water into a bucket, and brought it back to the living room. She looked at the two girls as she vigorously wiped down the floor with a wet cloth. "I heard your mother's down with weak lungs, so I was half-expecting her girls to be sallow and weak too. But look at you two—you couldn't be rosier. And smart, by the look of you.

"You know, this house was built for someone like your mother to rest and get well. A long time ago, when I was a girl, I was a maid in the house of a big landowner. The missus, she had the same problem as your mother. Her husband built this house for her.

"You see, Shichikokuyama Hospital is not far away, and it's famous for helping folks with TB. And I was very close to the missus. I worked hard and we got along well. I think she chose Matsugo because this is where I live."

When Tatsuo had visited to ask about renting the house, Mrs. Ogaki had been doubtful. Her employer had died there nearly twenty years before, and since then it had been empty. The forest had come to overshadow the house and its once well-tended garden, and it seemed to grow more dismal, shabby, and forlorn with each passing year. No wonder the children passing by on their way to school called it the haunted house.

"Your wife has lung problems too, does she?" she'd said to Tatsuo. "Well, I hope the house does her good. But I can't promise."

Now the old woman was almost finished wiping the floor. "Can I ask you about the soot sprites?" Satsuki said.

"Are they about this big?" Satsuki held a thumb and forefinger an inch or so apart. "Round, like dust balls? Hairy, like caterpillars?"

Granny got to her feet slowly and for a moment was lost in thought.

"They ran away quick, you said? When I saw 'em, they were off before I could blink my eyes."

"Do they run away like they're scared?" Satsuki said.

"That they do."

"Really fast?"

"Like a B-29, zooming away."

"You mean they can fly?"

"Of course they fly. Didn't you see 'em?"

As she was answering Satsuki's questions, Granny moved back and forth between the living room and the kitchen, putting away the pots and pans and cooking utensils. Satsuki followed close behind, and Mei stuck to Satsuki, sucking her thumb and clutching her sister's skirt, following right along but saying not a word.

Mei stuck to Satsuki like glue. There was something about the old woman's familiarity—not unusual, for country people—that Mei didn't like. Granny was very wrinkly and dark from the sun, and she had a big wart over one of her eyes. She was different in every way from gentle, well-mannered Grandmother Terashima.

"The older the house is, the more those soot sprites get settled in, and the more of them there are." Granny pretended Mei wasn't there. She knew that was the quickest way to make friends with shy little girls.

"Do they like houses that are falling apart?" asked Satsuki.

"Falling apart, and with nobody livin' in 'em."

"Are they ghosts?"

"Maybe not ghosts. They're spooky, though."

"Has anyone ever caught one?"

"That I don't know."

"But you've seen them, haven't you?" said Satsuki eagerly.

"I have."

"That's why you know all about them. When did you see them?"

"Oh, when I was about the same age as Little Miss Somebody behind you."

"Where? Was it in this house?"

The old woman chuckled and ran her fingers, with skin like dried, cracked mud, through her sparse white hair. "No. In those days this place was just thickets and trees, like the rest of the Tsukamori Woods. No soot sprites, just a lot of big tiger mosquitoes."

Mei was about to burst. She took her thumb out of her mouth and said, "So where did you see them?"

"In the house where my grandmother, and her grandmother, and her grandmother's grandmother grew up." The old woman beamed at Mei, but Mei planted her thumb back in her mouth and half hid behind Satsuki again, clutching her skirt.

## 2. Is the House Haunted?

Four o'clock came and went. Five o'clock came and went.

The room Tatsuo had chosen for his study was the Western-style addition built on to the house. Now the floor was piled with bundles of books in Japanese and English, long-unopened boxes with Tatsuo's collection of artifacts, and a scratched and scuffed old trunk.

The other rooms had been tidied up. The attic room over the study, reached by a narrow flight of stairs, was empty, but the rest of the house had been made livable. There was the front entryway, the toilet off the hall, the earthen-floored kitchen, and the living room where they would take their meals. Two more tatami rooms looked out over the garden.

"Daddy, let's give Mommy the room with the alcove," said Satsuki.

When the sun was low in the sky, and he was

satisfied that he'd helped out as much as he could, Uncle Fujiyama had turned the three-wheeler for home.

*Vroom, vroom. Putt putter-putt, putt putt putt putt…*

"Goodbye!" "Take care!" Satsuki was sorry Uncle Fujiyama wouldn't be staying the night.

Then Granny left, carrying an empty wicker basket on her back. "Be sure to visit us, now!" she said to Satsuki and Mei.

"See you soon!" "Thanks for helping out!"

Tatsuo, Mei, and Satsuki stood in the road next to the little bridge and waved goodbye as Granny's rounded back got slowly smaller and the dusk came down quietly across the forest and fields.

Wagging its tail and barking, a white dog came running toward Granny from the direction of her house.

A gust of wind blew little spinners of dust along the road.

Granny stopped where the road curved out of sight, turned, and waved one last time. Satsuki could see her scolding the dog as it jumped up to lick her face.

Satsuki waved back. "Goodbye! Come see us

again!" Mei stood quietly with her hands behind her back. For someone as shy with strangers as she was, waving goodbye to someone she'd just met today was impossible.

Tatsuo looked down at the girls. "Well, shall we get back?"

"Are we spending the night here?" Mei looked doubtful.

"That's right."

"Forever?"

"Sure. We moved today, didn't we? We're not just spending the night. This is our home now."

"Oh…"

The stream gurgled cheerfully at their feet. Nothing stirred along the road to the village and in the fields. Satsuki heard a distant rumble in the sky.

"All right, back we go," said Tatsuo.

The three of them crossed the stone footbridge and climbed the path to the yard, Satsuki leading the way, Tatsuo with Mei by the hand.

"Watch out there." Mei's foot caught on a tree root snaking across the path in the half light. Tatsuo lifted her up over it. "We'd better remember this is here."

"Yep, someone could trip on that," Satsuki

said. She scampered back and forth as they walked up the path.

"You don't look like you'd trip over anything," said Tatsuo.

"Don't worry about me," Satsuki said, laughing. "I can see even when it's pitch dark."

They walked on a little way in silence. Then Satsuki said, "It really is getting dark."

The overgrown garden's trees and bushes and hummocks of grass were nothing but black shapes against the last traces of light in the sky. A pale crescent moon floated above the forest. The giant laurel tree rose above the trees, stretching its black branches wide against the sky like a solemn sentinel. What was it waiting for?

"I'm hungry," Mei said.

Little Mei looked suddenly miserable. She was worn out from the long day of moving and hadn't had a rest since early morning.

"When we get back, I'll lay the futon out for you," Satsuki said. "Why don't you take a nap?"

"I don't want a nap." She had barely eaten any of the afternoon snacks Kanta had brought over to the house from his mother. Mei had just shaken her head at the mountains of pickled radish, rice cakes, and other home-cooked food. All she'd eaten was a grilled rice ball with a little miso spread on it, and then only because Satsuki had insisted. Mei was always shy and wary when strangers were around.

Now Satsuki felt an urge to tease Mei a little. "Daddy, how many rice cakes did we eat?"

"Stop talking about rice cakes," Mei said and broke into tears. She was ready for bed.

"Don't worry," said Tatsuo. "We'll get dinner going right away."

Satsuki suddenly remembered the soot sprites. What if they were still in the house? She crept up to the front door, took hold of the knob, and jerked it open.

The house was empty.

Inside, nothing moved.

Everything was silent and dim. Uncle Fujiyama's broad shoulders and Granny's voice, dispensing advice and instructions, were gone.

There was nothing but the three of them and the haunted house of Matsugo.

"I'll heat the bath, Daddy. The tub's full already," Satsuki said cheerfully. She slipped off her sneakers and took them along as she stepped up into the house.

"There's firewood in the kitchen," said Tatsuo.

"Maybe we should've collected more while it was still light."

"Don't worry. There's more in the corner of the garden. We made a pile after lunch."

"We? Oh, you mean you and Kanta?"

"Yup."

"Are you two friends now?"

"Nope," Satsuki said.

Kanta had wanted to go home after delivering the snacks, but Granny had instructed him to help Satsuki stock the woodpile. Satsuki couldn't get much out of him other than "Mm-hm," "Uh-uh," "Here" and "There." As soon as he'd completed his task, he turned suddenly and said, "Your house gives me the creeps. It's haunted. Can't you tell?" And he ran away.

Tatsuo chuckled. "Didn't go so well, I gather."

"He's really weird. Those short pants are way too big for him. It's not even summer yet and he's already brown." Satsuki frowned. "I mean, we haven't even had a fight and he doesn't like me. I think he's a big bully."

Satsuki marched straight-legged down the corridor toward the kitchen, banging her feet on the floor. "He'll just! Have to learn! Some manners! From Satsuki Kusakabe!"

Tatsuo, laughing, followed behind her. "Better watch out. The kids around here are used to lots of hard farm work. I bet he's no pushover, even for you."

"Don't you worry about me." Satsuki smiled. She dropped her shoes onto the floor of the kitchen and slipped them on again.

*Don't worry, Daddy. Make way for Satsuki Kusakabe, superstar! Ha ha ha ha!*

The firebox for the bathtub faced into the kitchen, in a square recess in the floor. Satsuki looked down at it and declared, "Time to get that fire going! First, we need some firewood."

She opened the back door. The darkness had deepened. A whistling seemed to come down from the sky.

The grass in the yard streamed in the wind.

"Let's see, I think it was over there." She stepped out into the yard.

The dense stand of trees that marked the edge of the forest ran along one side of the garden. Kanta and Satsuki had built a little pile of firewood close to the trees, just as Granny had instructed.

Satsuki crept past the well. She stepped on a little patch of evening primrose, its purple flowers blooming meekly in the dark. "Sorry," she said nervously, and hurried on.

The wind seemed to be getting stronger, moaning quietly through the trees.

Satsuki broke into a run for the woodpile.

The sky was filled with swiftly drifting clouds that were even blacker than the night. The moon, which had been weakly gleaming in the sky above her, was blotted out.

A gust of wind snapped a branch off a tree. It hurtled past her.

"Oh!"

Now the wind was blowing hard. *Hurry up, Satsuki.*

The bushes hissed in the darkness. Everything she could see was moving to and fro.

Another gust struck the thickets beyond the garden, startling the birds from sleep. Their frightened chirping rose above the sound of the wind.

"I don't like this," Satsuki said to the garden. The wind whipped the grass and the stems of plants against her legs.

*Gooooooooooooh...*

The wind seemed to be cutting a path high through the ashen sky. Something howled along that path, like a solid fist of wind glinting with sinister light. It groaned as it passed overhead.

Satsuki reached the pile and hastily gathered up an armful of wood. As she turned to go, the fist of wind swooped down and circled her in a whirlwind that tugged fiercely at her firewood and made the grass and twigs dance at her feet.

Then, with a peal of savage, ghostly laughter that rippled toward the four corners of the yard, the wind shot into the sky toward the crescent moon. It tore the firewood from her arms and sent it flying in a spiraling cloud of twigs and leaves toward the crown of the huge laurel. The laurel's branches shook violently in the wind, and the tree rasped and groaned as if its giant trunk were ready to split right down the middle. The frenzy in the sky was reaching a peak.

*Firewood. I can't go back without the firewood.* Satsuki pulled herself together and ran back to the woodpile, still fighting the wind. She knelt and gathered up as much wood as she could carry. The branches jabbed her painfully, but this was no time to be choosy. She gritted her teeth and hugged the wood tightly. She could see the back door. Now *run*.

The wind rose into the sky and swooped down at her, again and again.

At last she reached the back door, but before bolting through it, she turned, trembling, toward the laurel. Its enormous bulk loomed over the forest, writhing in the wind, a deeper black against the dark sky.

How many years had it taken to grow so tall?

*Maybe it's always been here*, thought Satsuki. *It must know everything about this village. And even if there are monsters in the bushes and something awful flying around in the sky, there isn't anything that could scare that tree.*

She put the firewood by the back door, stood up straight, and faced the tree. She had decided it was time to say something to this giant sentinel that stood watch over their house.

"I need you to do something for us," she said in a solemn voice. "I'm sure you'll be here when we're gone. But until then, we need your protection. Please don't forget us."

The tree must have understood. How could it not have heard what she said?

Satsuki decided the laurel was nodding its branches back at her. She made up her mind that things would be all right.

She opened the door and went into the kitchen. Tatsuo was at the wood-fired hearth, busily preparing dinner. "Did you get some more wood? The wind sure is loud."

"Yeah, I wasn't ready for it. It's blowing really hard."

After the yard, the kitchen felt snug and safe. Satsuki carried the wood over to the firebox. "Where's Mei?"

"Out like a light."

"Good. Did you tuck her in?"

"Mm-hmm. She burrowed right into the futon. I guess she was really worn out."

"Is she in Mommy's room?" That was what Satsuki had decided to call the eight-mat room with the alcove.

"Mm-hmm."

"Well, it's good she's asleep."

"Yep, that gives us more time to get ready. When Mei starts crying, everything comes to a stop."

"I know."

Time to get ready.

Satsuki looked at her thumb, which was bleeding from the sharp end of a piece of wood. "I better light the fire, I guess."

"That's a good idea. I wonder if Mei will want to take a bath tonight."

"She has to. She's all dusty."

"You're right. It's a pain to light the fire, though."

"I'll take care of it."

"Thank you kindly."

"You just be the cook tonight, Daddy," Satsuki said. "I'll take care of the bath. All I have to do is follow Granny's instructions."

Satsuki gathered up all the old newspaper they had used to pack the dishes. She found a box of matches and put the wood within easy reach.

"Daddy, this should be enough newspaper to get a fire going, right?"

Tatsuo looked at the pile of newspaper. He was an experienced hiker and often built campfires in the mountains. "You might need more than that."

"Really? Okay, I'll get some more."

Satsuki was completely new at this. She turned to the firebox. This was going to be fun.

She squatted down like a seasoned fire-lighter in the little pit, facing the firebox. She was nervous, but that was fun too. She picked up each of the tools propped against the side of the pit and looked at them—the poker, the tongs, and the little tin dustpan for cleaning out the ash.

She lit one piece of newspaper. It quickly burst

into flame. Startled, she stuffed it through the fire-box door as fast as she could. That was hot!

"Okay, Daddy, I'm lighting the fire." Satsuki started wadding up big balls of newspaper.

"You look very determined," Tatsuo said, chuckling. He was opening a can of dried sardines.

"That's right. Granny said everything depends on how you set things up."

First the newspaper, then put in some dry twigs, and firewood on top, stacked so it will burn well. Set it up the right way from the beginning and you'll be fine. That's what Granny had told her. But the twigs refused to burn.

"Daddy?"

"Mm-hmm."

"What are you doing?"

"Getting the sardines ready."

"For miso soup?"

"You're absolutely right."

The twigs and firewood wouldn't seem to burn. They just smoldered and smoked, and the smoke wasn't going up the chimney. It was coming into the kitchen.

"Satsuki?"

"What?"

"Are you sad about something?"

Satsuki coughed, laughed and coughed again. "I'm fine." Her eyes were watering from the smoke. Now even the newspaper was going out.

It was almost as if the fire was playing hide and seek. Every now and then, there would be a sharp hiss. A lovely tongue of flame would dart up, and for a moment she could see the inside of the old firebox. The floor of the firebox was a grate of rusty iron bars.

"Daddy, there's a grate for the ash to fall through." The walls of the firebox were concrete and full of cracks. "Hey, I see a bug! Now it's gone." The fire leaped up, then smoldered and smoked again.

Satsuki closed the firebox door, waited a little, then opened it again. The burning wood had a wonderful fragrance.

"Doesn't it smell nice, Daddy?" Satsuki was entranced.

She tried twisting the newspaper more tightly. She moved the firewood around. She was learning.

By now the fire should have been burning warmly and throwing off a nice red glow. But lighting the fire for a bath is tricky. As Satsuki watched the flames struggling, she realized how hard it was going to be.

Tatsuo was watching and smiling. Now and then he poked fun at her gently, but he didn't offer to help.

"Satsuki?"

"Yes, Dad."

"How's it going?"

"It's fun."

"Glad to hear it's fun. Is the water in the bathtub any warmer than before?"

"Ha ha ha. You're mean."

It wasn't going well at all, but Satsuki was determined. She still didn't have a proper fire, her cheeks were hot from peering into the firebox, and the smoke kept going up her nose. The fire threatened to go out completely, but she watched carefully. She was going to get this right.

"Well, let's see," said Tatsuo. "What did Granny say? First you hear the metal bathtub rumbling and flexing. Then when the fizzing sound starts and keeps going, close the damper halfway, but don't take the lid off the bath for anything. Wait a minute…does the fizzing come before the rumbling? Now I can't remember."

Tatsuo put the knife down, lost in thought. *I guess we're really living here now*, he said to himself.

Yasuko would surely be happy to be reunited with her family. But would living here really help her recover? Wouldn't it be better for her to be back in Tokyo? And until she came home, could the three of them manage on their own?

"All right. Are we going to eat this, or should I just toss it out?" Tatsuo said.

"That won't work," said a voice behind him. Satsuki looked up to see Kanta Ogaki coming through the back door. He came and stood behind her. "That won't work," he said again.

He turned to Tatsuo and gave him a dozen eggs, tied up in paper. "This is from Grandma."

"Well, thanks a lot," said Tatsuo. "Do they always keep you this busy?"

Kanta shrugged and looked at the firebox again. "Got a hatchet?"

"What's a hatchet?" Satsuki said. "You mean like an axe?"

Without answering, Kanta kept his usual frown in place and looked around the kitchen until he spotted the hatchet under the sink. He took a piece of firewood, stood it on end, and split it clean down the center. He did this until he had a pile of kindling.

"Nice technique," said Tatsuo.

"I do this every day."

"Your family must depend on you."

Kanta kept the frown, but his face turned red. He picked up the kindling and held it out to Satsuki. "I'll show you."

He squatted in front of the firebox next to Satsuki. "Matches?" he said, rather self-importantly.

"Here you go." Satsuki handed him the box of matches.

Kanta studied the box. "Hey, there's a picture of a peach."

"They're from the fruit parlor. They give them away."

Kanta looked puzzled. He'd never heard of a "fruit parlor." Anyway, who cared what it was? It didn't have anything to do with lighting a fire properly.

Trying to be helpful, Satsuki wadded up some sheets of newspaper.

"You're wasting it," said Kanta. "One or two is enough."

"Really? I must've used thirty or forty, but it won't light."

"You're new at this." Kanta smiled shyly. He was trying to make Satsuki feel better.

Satsuki had no idea why this bad-tempered boy had turned suddenly friendly, but as she watched him skillfully arranging the kindling, she forgot her puzzlement. The flames leaped up.

"Hey, you got it going!" Satsuki clapped her hands in delight.

"That should do it." Kanta made sure the fire was moving from the kindling to the logs. Then he shut the firebox with a clang.

"Listen now, don't open the door again for a while, or the fire will go out."

"Okay. Oh, it's so pretty." The fire glowed through the little window in the firebox. "Listen to it pop!"

"That's the cedar."

"How do you know it's cedar?"

" 'Cause of the smell."

Satsuki was impressed. But next time she was going to do it herself, no matter what. She had learned a lot. She was sure she could do it next time.

"Dinner's on," said Tatsuo. "Better go wake up Mei. Why don't you stay for dinner with us, Kanta?"

"Oh, no thanks." Kanta shook his head. Now that the fire was going, he was back to his stand-offish self. "See you!" he mumbled, and ran out the back door.

The night was pitch black now. The wind kept blowing. As it boomed against the house, the old building answered with creaks and rattles and groans of its own. Even things inside the house were murmuring to the wind. The cupboard doors rattled softly.

"The wind is really loud!" Mei sat in the steaming water, looking red as a boiled octopus. "Daddy, is the house going to fall down? It's so old."

Tatsuo relaxed in the steaming water. "Well, I hope not. We just moved in." He smiled. Their long day was finally ending.

They had moved all the way from Tokyo. Everyone had eaten. Now they were having a nice hot bath. All that was left was to go to bed. And tomorrow was Sunday. They could sleep in.

A big gust thudded against the house. Everything shook. Something rattled and banged over their heads.

"This is getting scary," said Satsuki, soaping herself next to the tub.

"What was that noise, Daddy?" Mei said.

"Just the wind."

"But something was banging." Satsuki was so

nervous, she jumped into the bath still covered with suds.

Kanta had said the house was haunted. He said it gave him the creeps.

"Must be the kitchen," said Tatsuo. "The roof's tin."

"Why would the roof make noise?"

"Because the wind is trying to blow it off."

"What should we do?" Satsuki looked worried.

"Nothing. Stop fretting."

"I heard something go bang in the yard. What was it, Daddy?" asked Mei.

"Probably the buckets next to the well."

"I'll go get them after we're finished," Satsuki said. "If they blow away, we can't carry water."

"Good thinking," said Tatsuo lazily. "If we don't bring them back, the goblins of Tsukamori Woods might make off with them. Then we'd have a real problem."

*Hoo hoo…Hoo hoo…*

Satsuki looked at the ceiling nervously. "Daddy, was that a goblin?"

*Hoo hoo hoo…*

"There it is again!"

"Relax. It's just an owl. The forest is probably full of them. We'll just have to get used to it."

*Now how are we going to get from here to our beds in Mommy's room down that dark hall?* Satsuki thought.

"Daddy, let's all get out of the bath together. We should all go to sleep together. You don't have to work anymore today, do you?"

Tatsuo laughed. "What are we going to tell your Mother tomorrow? She'll think we're a bunch of scaredy cats."

## 3. Mother

When Satsuki opened her eyes next morning, she felt very odd. As she lay in the futon, the feeling wouldn't go away.

Everything seemed so different. The room was so large. It was dark too, until she noticed a little circle of sunlight on the floor next to her pillow. Sunlight was streaming through a knothole in the shutter. Peering through it, she could see blurry trees outside.

There was an old pond in the garden, now just a few shallow puddles. The grass grew thick where the rest of the water used to be. Next to it was a staircase of stone slabs that went to the top of a little hummock. Had they climbed it yesterday?

There was a stone footbridge. Wasn't there a little stream running under it?

One by one, Satsuki remembered different things about this new place she had woken up in.

And then, of course, she remembered the best thing of all.

"Mei! Mei! C'mon, let's get up!"

Mei was sprawled on her back on her futon, arms and legs spread in all directions. Satsuki gave her a shove. "Mei, we have to get going. We're going to see Mommy today. Let's hurry!"

"Mmm…"

As soon as she heard the word "Mommy," Mei rolled over and got up on all fours. She rubbed her eyes. "Where's Daddy?"

Come to think of it, where was he? Tatsuo's futon was next to Mei's. It was folded neatly.

"He's up already. I wonder where he is." Satsuki opened the sliding glass door and pushed the shutter to one side. It was a beautiful Sunday morning.

The wind from the day before must have taken all the clouds for miles around and swept them far away. The sky was crystalline blue. The giant laurel rose toward the sky. It was very still. Not a leaf was moving.

Satsuki and Mei hurried to get dressed. They ran into the living room, then the kitchen, but nothing had been touched from the night before. They'd have to clean up!

"Daddy! Daddy!"

"Where are you?"

They ran back down the hall and opened the door to the study. The room was just like Tatsuo's study in Tokyo—piles of new and old books scattered all over, with an armchair in the center.

"I see you're up." Tatsuo was reading a book. Its cover had turned brown with age. He stood up and stretched.

"We get to see Mommy today, don't we?" Satsuki said.

"That's right. She must be looking forward to seeing us."

"When can we leave? What time is it now?"

"In another fifteen minutes, it will be ten o'clock. Let's go after we have breakfast and do a little laundry."

"But it'll be late then!"

"I don't want breakfast," Mei said.

"We can't just go anytime we want. The hospital has rules too. It's Sunday, so visiting hours start at one o'clock. If we take care of the chores first, we'll be right on time. It'll take us less than an hour to get there on the bicycle."

When they lived in Tokyo, they had to walk

from the house to the station, get on a train, then change to another train, ride for a long time, get off and wait forever for a local train, then get off *that* train and take a bus to the hospital.

"Daddy, isn't it great that we moved?" Satsuki jumped onto the lawn in her bare feet. "Come on, Mei, let's wash our faces at the pump!"

No matter how long it took to get to the hospital, any day that included a visit to Mother was a happy day. But today was even more special.

The weather was beautiful, and for the first time they were taking the bicycle. And now they'd be able to see her much more often, because the house was so close!

Suddenly Satsuki remembered the acorns. They'd have to tell Yasuko about their haunted house. She put her hand in her pocket and felt for the acorn. It was still there.

"Hmm?" Satsuki looked at the little round acorn with surprise. It had changed color.

"Mei, do you still have your acorns?"

"From yesterday? Mm-hmm."

"Can I take a look?"

Mei groped in the pocket of her dress. "There's one...There's the other one."

Mei's acorns were the same brown color as

Satsuki's. "So yours changed color too. That's strange. They were green yesterday," Satsuki said.

"Maybe they got rotten."

"They're not rotten, just brown. Let's take these to Mommy. We'd better tell her there's spooks in the house." She put Mei's acorns in her pocket and began walking round and round the well.

"What are you doing?" Mei was puzzled.

"Thinking!"

*We moved in*, she thought, *and the sprites moved out. Soot sprites won't stay in a house with people. And neither will spooks. That's what Granny said.*

"Are you scared of us?" Satsuki spoke to the garden in a low voice, so Mei wouldn't hear. "Where do you go?"

Something passed through the flowers and grass behind her, as if to answer. It was like a faint puff of wind.

Maybe it was an insect in a hurry to get somewhere. Maybe it was something watching them. Satsuki wasn't sure.

Then again, even if she wasn't sure, if what moved through the grass just now was some kind of spirit, what did it want them to do?

Stay or go?

Satsuki tossed her short, wavy hair and said, "Mommy will help us decide."

"Decide what?" Mei said. She worked the pump handle idly up and down.

"What to do if our house is really haunted."

The breakfast dishes had all been washed and put away and the laundry hung out to dry, but Tatsuo didn't seem in a hurry to get going.

"Daddy, aren't we going?" Mei said.

"If we don't leave soon we'll be late!" Satsuki said.

"Hold on, there. We have to lock up the house," said Tatsuo. "Wait a minute—I left my cap on the desk in the study. I'll go get it."

"You better not start reading a book, Daddy!"

Satsuki's patience had run out. They were supposed to hurry.

"Of course not," Tatsuo said. He laughed happily.

Satsuki looked terribly serious. "But you're not even trying to hurry!"

"All right, all right."

At last it was time to go. Once he was on the bicycle, Tatsuo was impatient to get moving.

"Look at this weather. The laundry will be dry in no time. Mei, put that strap under your chin or you'll lose your bonnet."

"Okay!"

"Satsuki! Canteen filled?"

"Yes sir!"

Mei sat in front of Tatsuo on a cushion tied to the bicycle frame with string to make a little saddle. Satsuki stood on the rear wheel rack with the canteen slung over one shoulder.

"Here we go!" said Tatsuo. "Satsuki, maybe you better sit while we ride down the front path."

"I'll be fine."

"I hope so." Tatsuo wasn't sure that Satsuki might not fall off the back of the bicycle on the way down. Yet as he started off, he steered the front wheel all over the place and made the girls scream with suspense.

They flew down the path, through the gate, and across the bridge. Mei looked down at the little stream running next to the road.

"I wish we had a fish for Mommy."

"Yes, that would've been nice," said Tatsuo. He was pedaling energetically along the road. "The brook must be full of them."

"Can you eat 'em?" asked Satsuki.

"Why not? But first you've got to catch 'em."

"That's out, then," said Satsuki from her perch behind Tatsuo. "The fish swim really fast. They run away when you get close, way too fast to catch."

She leaned over Tatsuo's shoulder. "Daddy? I bet Kanta could catch one."

Kanta knew where to find the best firewood. He could use a hatchet to split kindling, and he knew how to build a fire in the furnace. Probably he could do just about anything, Satsuki decided.

The sky was reflected in the brown water of the paddies. Some of them were already full of green rice shoots. Others were waiting to be planted. Farmers wearing rubber boots bent over as they planted the seedlings.

"Let's find Granny!" Mei said.

"Let's find Kanta!" Satsuki said.

They kept an eye out for Granny and Kanta. As they rode past a field of canola plants, Mei tried to touch the flowers. She couldn't reach them, but she loved to try.

"Look, there's Granny!" Satsuki called. "Granny Ogaaaakiiii!"

Quite a distance away in one of the paddies, three figures stood up slowly. They were wearing straw hats.

"Hello!"

Tatsuo stopped the bicycle and took off his cap. "Mrs. Ogaki! Thanks for all your help yesterday!"

Granny Ogaki and Kanta's mother and father bowed, then bowed again. And again. A little boy next to them gave a friendly wave. He must have been Kanta's brother.

"Where are you off to?" Kanta's mother called out.

"The hospital!" Mei shouted as loud as she could. And she'd been so quiet yesterday!

"Whaaat?" called Granny.

"The hos-pi-taaal! To see Mo-ther!" Satsuki called back.

"Whaaat?"

Maybe they couldn't hear, but the figures in the paddy kept waving as Tatsuo started off again.

A little further down the road, Kanta came climbing up from the fields. He had a pole balanced on his shoulders with an empty basket at either end. As Satsuki passed him, standing up on the back of the bicycle, he stuck his tongue out so hard, his face turned red. Satsuki turned and stuck her tongue out too. And off they went, in opposite directions!

It couldn't be helped. They were both feeling shy. Kanta didn't know how to talk to Satsuki yet. Satsuki was thankful that Kanta had helped her light the fire, but she felt a little self-conscious about needing his help.

It was May.

The earth, still damp from the spring rains, seemed to sigh, exhaling a sweet mist toward the clear blue heavens.

The bicycle raced along the hard-packed road, throwing little stones to either side. The paddies and fields shimmered in the soft light. The wind ruffled their hair. Tatsuo started to sing.

"May and May, riding along in May…"

"Daddy, what do you think Uncle Fujiyama is doing today?" Mei said.

"Working his fields, I suppose."

"He must be pretty busy at this time of year," Satsuki said.

"Daddy?" asked Mei.

"Mm-hm?"

"How come Uncle Fujiyama doesn't teach at the university like you?"

"He took over the family farm. He's the eldest son. He doesn't have time to teach."

"But you work together sometimes," Satsuki

said. "Doing excavations, or whatever you call them."

"That's because he's a virtuoso with the shovel."

"Don't you know how to use a shovel too?"

"Sure, but I'm not very good at it. I'm better at using a pen and writing reports."

They arrived at the edge of the village and crossed a wooden bridge over a deep gully. The water at the bottom plashed merrily over the stones in the streambed. The sides of the gully were thick with the bright brown trunks of cedar trees.

Tatsuo kept pedaling, one passenger in front and another behind. He was getting soaked with perspiration.

After what seemed like quite a long time, they saw a statue of Jizo, the guardian of children, at a fork in the road. Tatsuo was out of breath. He stopped by a pine tree. Satsuki and Mei jumped down.

"Whew. I'm tired," said Tatsuo. He lay down in the grass and stretched his arms and legs. "Dead tired. I thought it was closer than this."

Satsuki and Mei went to look at the little stone figure decked out in his red cloth bib and cap. Right nearby they found a little wooden sign reading SHORTCUT TO SHICHIKOKUYAMA HOSPITAL.

"There's a shortcut, Daddy! If we go this way, we'll get there faster."

"A shortcut?" Tatsuo was doubtful. "It looks pretty steep. What about the other road?"

"It goes through a forest," said Satsuki, craning her neck to see down the road.

"You can do it, Daddy," Mei said.

They all had a drink of water from the canteen and decided to try the shortcut. It was getting close to one o'clock.

The shortcut did look like it might be quicker, but gradually it began to look more like a trail than a road. It ran like a thread toward the ridge of Mount Haké. The slopes were covered by thick stands of bamboo grass. The path was so narrow and steep that they had to walk.

As they went along, butterflies scattered and flew away on either side. The straight, tall trunks of cedars were covered with ivy vines. The leaves were small and pretty, but the vines were too tough for even Satsuki to break, no matter how hard she tugged. They also gave off an unpleasant smell, like a squashed bug.

It was hard going on the steep path. They often had to stop and catch their breath. As they walked slowly upward, they began to wonder whether they should have taken the other fork after all. But it was too late for that now.

Gradually the pine trees started to close in. They had to be careful not to trip over the roots that stuck up here and there in the middle of the path.

The girls sat down on a big pine root and waited for Tatsuo to catch up. He couldn't go as fast as Satsuki and Mei because he had the bicycle to push up the trail.

"Wait up, you little imps," Tatsuo said. "Please don't throw any acorns at me."

But they were in luck, for the path they had taken was a shortcut after all. When they reached the top and looked down the other side, they could see the red roof of the sanatorium through the pines.

They hurried down the steep path cut into the slope and marched through the wooden gate. The sliding doors to the lobby creaked noisily.

It was crowded in the lobby. On Sundays, the sanatorium was always full of relatives and friends of the patients.

"You two go ahead and find your mother," said Tatsuo as he filled out a visiting form at the reception desk.

"What about you, Daddy?"

"I'll say hello to the doctor first. You don't want to wait around for that, do you?"

"Nope. See you later." Satsuki felt a little nervous. She took Mei firmly by the hand and started off down the long corridor toward the women's ward.

The corridor always seemed very dreary and gloomy. The floor creaked, and the slippers they had to change into were too big for children. They made a loud noise as they slapped on the wooden floor.

The corridor was always crowded with patients and visitors. Satsuki didn't like the way the patients glanced at her and Mei as they walked past the sick rooms. It made her feel lonely somehow.

Worst of all, this was the men's ward. They had to pass through it to get to Mother's room. It couldn't be helped, but for Satsuki, the men's ward was a scary place.

The skinny man in the long, loose dressing gown, standing at the window with a sidelong smile.

The old man with trembling hands, slowly eating the box lunch his wife brought for him.

The man in pajamas holding a cup of steaming

liquid as he walked. His cheeks were so hollow, his face looked like a skull.

And the strange, heavy smell.

The sickroom doors were open. Beyond them, they could see rows of iron cots. In some of them men lay very still, as if too weak to move.

*What if Mommy ends up like that?*

Everything in these rooms seemed listless and still. The chrysanthemums in the vases on the wall, the strings of origami cranes hanging from the ceiling…

Satsuki tugged at Mei's hand. They weren't supposed to run, but little by little they did. They wanted to get out of there as soon as they could.

The women's ward always seemed so much brighter and more cheerful. Was it because Mom was there? But when they got to the door, Satsuki started to worry. What if she wasn't?

Mom never seemed to be in her room when they came to visit. It was so embarrassing having to stand at the foot of her empty bed waiting and waiting, while patients in the other beds looked at them.

Satsuki slid open the door. There she was, right where she was supposed to be, waiting for them! Yasuko was sitting on her bed next to the window, wearing a pretty indigo half-coat with a pattern of flowers over her robe.

Satsuki and Mei smiled at her. Her eyes twinkled and the corners of her mouth dimpled into a smile.

There were six beds in the ward room. The patients greeted them warmly.

"Well, look who's here."

"You've come such a long way."

Mei ran to her mother, half sliding across the floor thanks to her big slippers. Yasuko looked steadily at Satsuki with her large eyes and motioned her to come. She gave Mei a hug.

"We moved into the new old house," said Mei and hugged her back.

"You must be tired." Yasuko kept one arm around Mei and drew Satsuki toward her with the other. Her fingers were long and slender, but her hands were strong. "Come." Her voice had a quiet strength of its own.

"Your mother's been waiting for you since early this morning," Yasuko said. "I kept wondering when you'd come. I was starting to get tired. Why did it take you so long?"

"We were straightening up the house," Satsuki said. "We did the laundry too."

As she spoke, Satsuki looked at her mother. Yasuko's long hair was parted in the middle and gathered in the back.

She cocked her head and smiled. She didn't look sick at all. "I'm so happy you came to see me."

"Daddy's coming too. He's talking to the doctor."

"Good." Yasuko ran her fingers through Satsuki's hair. Then she gave her daughter a quick hug. Yasuko was a graceful, slender woman who always smelled faintly of honeysuckle. Before she fell ill, she had always been busy and full of energy, and went everywhere with her head held high.

Suddenly Satsuki remembered how her mother looked and sounded when she was mad. And just as suddenly, the memory made her feel safe and comforted. She laughed out loud.

"Satsuki?" Yasuko looked at her solemnly. "I heard the house is old. Did you get everything moved in?"

"Mostly, mm-hmm."

"It's got spooks," Mei said. "But I'm okay. They don't scare me."

"Do you think you'll be able to manage, just the three of you? Until I come home?"

"Yes, we'll be fine," Satsuki said. "I think we can manage somehow."

"Things were so much easier in Tokyo. Yoné and Fumi were always there to help." Yoné and Fumi were the Terashima family's nanny and housekeeper.

"I know. That's why Daddy said he's going to find someone to help us out."

"That would be nice," said Yasuko. "Otherwise, our pretty little baby will be all alone when Daddy's at the university and Satsuki's in school." Yasuko smiled and ran a finger down Mei's cheek.

"I'm okay," Mei said solemnly. "I'll guard the house till they come back."

"Really?" Yasuko's eyes twinkled. "That will be a big help. After all, we don't have much money."

"Housekeepers cost money?" Satsuki was surprised. She had always thought Yoné and Fumi were, well, not exactly members of the family, but part of the household, as if they had sprouted naturally, like the mushrooms in the garden.

"Of course they cost money," said Yasuko.

"Can't Daddy make it?"

"I don't think he can make very much."

"Why?"

"The university doesn't pay much."

"But he does translations. Doesn't he get money for that?" Satsuki was even more puzzled.

"He does, but don't forget that I'm sick, and he has to pay a lot of money to the hospital."

"Maybe we shouldn't have moved, Mommy." To Satsuki, this suddenly seemed the only solution. "Maybe we should tell Daddy we want to go back to Tokyo."

"We'll do no such thing." Yasuko looked at her sternly. "Don't even think that. It wouldn't be fun at all."

"Why?"

"Because I wouldn't be able to see you very often. And besides, we can't stay with your grandparents forever. We have to make our way on our own, like everyone else."

This made sense to Satsuki. "You're right." She nodded.

"Being able to have fun takes a lot of work, you know."

"I already found out." Mother and daughter looked at each other and laughed. Mei hugged Yasuko's neck and laughed merrily too.

"Your mother is very lucky. I envy her," said the white-haired woman in the next bed. She turned her head on the pillow to smile at Satsuki and Mei. "Children are so wonderful when they're little. My own children are all grown up."

The woman by the door added, "Be sure to get lots of kisses from your mother before you go home today."

Yasuko, Satsuki, and Mei looked at each other and laughed again.

"Oh now you see, that reminds me," said Yasuko. "I made a present for each of you. Would you like to see?"

"Yes!" said the girls in unison. They became so excited that Yasuko put a finger to her lips. She went to a small cupboard and brought back two small packages wrapped in blue paper.

"Which one's mine?" cried Mei.

"This is for you," said Yasuko. She put a fingertip to Mei's forehead and smiled. "There's a letter too. Your father or Satsuki can read it to you when you get home."

Mei's present was a cloth tote bag with a shoulder strap.

"You'll be five soon, won't you Mei? You're getting to be a big girl, so Mommy made something grown-up for you."

The light green bag was decorated with the

faces of a laughing little girl and a crying little boy, all done out in embroidery. The effect was quite stylish.

"You always have to be the grown-up, Satsuki, so your present is a little bit babyish."

Satsuki unwrapped her package. "Oh! Clothes for Anne!"

Anne was a porcelain doll that Satsuki treasured more than anything else. There was a matching skirt and blouse, two dresses, and even a little sweater knitted from cardigan yarn.

"When the nurses or patients found a nice piece of cloth, they gave it to me for Anne. Do you like the clothes?" asked Yasuko, looking very pleased herself.

"Of course I like them! They're just what I wanted."

Everyone was admiring the presents when the door opened a crack and Tatsuo peeked in. "Anyone home?"

Mei ran happily across the room to show Tatsuo her tote bag. Yasuko stood up next to Satsuki.

"You've gotten so big since I've been here," she sighed. Satsuki came up to her mother's shoulder. "I wonder what you'll be like when you grow up."

She smiled and sat down again. "I'm sure you'll be very lovely."

A grinning Tatsuo joined them holding Mei, who was laughing and kicking, in the air by both arms.

The three of them sang as they wound their way back home.

Yasuko could leave the hospital in the autumn, perhaps even earlier. "That's what the doctor says, so we can rely on it," Tatsuo had announced when they were all together.

Tatsuo sang one of his old school songs, and it went like this:

*The clouds o'er Kyoto are purple in spring,*
*And the straw banquet mats*
*Have a fragrance like flowers.*

Satsuki and Mei sang a children's song, and it went like this:

*The white goat sent a letter*
*But the black goat thought it better*
*To eat the white goat's letter*
*Than to read it.*

Mei looked up at the sky and called as loud as she could, "I won't eat Mommy's letter, 'cause I'm not a black goat! I'll never never ever eat Mommy's letter!"

And their happiness went on and on, even after they got home and were safe in their own beds.

## 4. Mei Meets Totoro

*To Miss Satsuki at the Haunted House*
*Tsukamori, Matsugo Village*

Satsuki was surprised by the address on the letter. She turned the envelope over and read the return address. It was from Mother.

*Dear Satsuki,*

*If you are reading this letter then it must have reached you.*

*Are you well? What are you up to? The last time we met, you told me you were living in a famous haunted house, so I decided to write you this letter and find out just how famous it really is.*

*If the house's reputation is as you say (I'm looking forward to coming home, too), I shouldn't even need to put your last name on the envelope. If I just write Princess Satsuki at the Haunted House, it should reach you.*

*But then again, I have a feeling it might be dangerous to write Princess Satsuki, because the postman might really think it was a joke.*

*After spending a year in the sanatorium, I've become good at finding pleasure and laughter in simple things. But I'm afraid I may be forgetting what common sense is all about, so I do have to be careful. And that's why I decided to write Miss instead of Princess.*

Did that count as being careful? wondered Satsuki.

*Now then, my precious, adorable, hard-working Satsuki.*

*If this letter reaches you, then our new house may really be haunted after all.*

*Just think, a haunted house!*

*Did you know your mother used to be a rather strange little girl? When people asked me what I liked best, well, most little girls would say "dolls" or something like that, don't you think? But I always said "ghosts." I really did, you know.*

*You remember the big cherry tree in the garden at the Terashima house, don't you? I often used to hide out there. This was when I was very small, mind you. I thought if I were to meet a ghost, out by the cherry tree was where I would probably meet one.*

She was right, thought Satsuki. That part of the garden was always a little spooky, with that old locked-up air-raid shelter.

*But I never met any ghosts in the garden. I think it was because the neighborhood has always had so many houses and so many people. There are no fields or forests or lonely places for ghosts to hide.*

*And now you've all moved to a house with ghosts! And you brought me acorns the ghost gave you!*

*I was so happy you brought them. Those little acorns remind me of you and Mei. I caress them every day and say good morning and good night and How are you? to them.*

Mommy really loves us a lot, Satsuki realized.

*I noticed something interesting about the houses people live in. If there's a spooky legend about the house, it looks legend-y. If it holds some kind of secret, it looks secret-y.*

*If there's a ghost, the house looks ghostly.*

*If a scholar lives in the house, the house looks scholarly.*

*Your father is an archaeologist, so after a while it will start to look that way. But right now it's still ghostly, I suppose.*

Satsuki couldn't decide. Was the house ghostly, or archaeology-ly?

*I hope I'll be able to come home while the house is still ghostly. I want to see what ghostly is like. I loved ghosts so much when I was little. I hope I can meet a real one.*

*I'd like you to do something for me.*

*If you do see a ghost, please be sure to tell it that I want to meet it. Please don't forget. Tell it not to go away.*

*Well, it's time for lights out. I hope you'll always be healthy and happy!*

*All my love to Mei. I'll write again,*

*Mother*

Satsuki smiled. *I won't forget, Mommy. If I meet a ghost, I'll be sure to tell him what you said,* she thought.

She put the letter back in the envelope and carefully put it in her schoolbag, along with the mail for Tatsuo that was waiting in the mailbox.

"Finished?" Miyoko called down from the top of the embankment. Satsuki was sitting on the footbridge, dangling her legs over the little stream.

Miyoko was Satsuki's classmate. Her house was near Mount Haké, on the other side of Matsui River, down the road that turned off before Satsuki's house. But on the way home from school she usually walked with Satsuki as far as the bridge.

"Finished. It was from my mom," Satsuki said.

"You're so lucky." Miyoko skipped and slid down the slope.

"What makes me lucky?"

"I mean, getting a letter from your mother."

"Why not? She's in the hospital."

"See? Lucky."

Satsuki giggled. Miyoko picked up her bag from where she left it on the bridge and put her arms through the straps. "See you tomorrow," she called cheerfully as she walked away.

"See you tomorrow." Satsuki started up the path to the house. Miyoko headed toward her usual shortcut across the paddies.

"Miss Moriyama says you can't stay home just 'cause it rains," she called again.

Satsuki laughed. "Too bad!"

"See you!"

"Bye! See you tomorrow!"

Satsuki walked around to the doors that opened onto the garden from the study and peeked in. Tatsuo was staring at a report he was writing. He was wearing his work frown. Satsuki decided to go in by the front door so as not to disturb him, but just as she was about to go he looked up and smiled.

"Hello there. Is it already that time of day?"

"I'm back." Satsuki came into the study and dropped her bag. "Boy, is that getting heavy. Daddy, what time is it?"

"The time? It's...two seventeen."

"Not quite snack time yet. Here's your mail. I guess I'll go write Mommy a letter. She sent me one. Where's Mei?"

Tatsuo glanced at the envelopes and looked

up. "She's out in the yard. Would you go take a look?"

"In the garden?" Satsuki walked into the yard.

"Mei! Mei! I'm home. Where are you? No hide and seek, okay? Mei!"

There was no answer. Maybe she was around the back. Satsuki walked to the back door, calling Mei's name.

But the yard was deserted. "That's strange," Satsuki said out loud.

She climbed up the hill to the bamboo grove that rose behind the house. Beyond the grove was an expanse of tea fields where they often went to play. Sometimes they sledded down the hill on straw mats.

"Mei! Mei!"

There was no one at the top. One of the straw mats lay in the grass. Now Satsuki was beginning to feel really worried.

"Daddy!"

She looked along the expanse of fields, furrowed and ready for planting, to Kanta's house in the distance beyond. Not a soul could be seen. Where in the world had Mei gotten to?

"Daddy, come out here!"

Tatsuo came around the house and looked up

at Satsuki. He still had his fountain pen in his hand, as if he expected Mei to make an appearance any moment so he could return to his writing. "Can't you find her?"

"No. She's not here!" Satsuki looked far out over the fields and forest. She could see the road that led to Miyoko's house and the bridge where it crossed the Matsui River.

She wasn't there. Well, of course not. Mei would never go that far from the house.

Satsuki ran back down the hill. Mei had to be somewhere near the house. That was the only thing that made sense.

Mei wouldn't start kindergarten for almost another year. So far she hadn't made a single friend. Since the family moved to Matsugo, she always played quietly in the house or out in the yard. She talked to herself constantly, usually in earshot of Tatsuo as he worked.

"Where could she be?" Tatsuo said. He was starting to look a bit pale. "Hold on, Satsuki. Let's do this systematically. Let me put my pen down." He ran back to the study.

*All he thinks about is work*, thought Satsuki. *Aunt Terashima used to complain about it all the time. And she was right.* She could feel herself getting angry with her father. She hadn't liked it when Auntie criticized him, but now she found herself agreeing with her.

*Work, work, work!* Was it so much to ask for him to check every now and then to see if Mei was all right?

Tatsuo came hopping back around the house. He was trying to run and put his shoes on at the same time. "What about the stream out front? Did you check there?"

"What for? I was sitting there just a few minutes ago."

"Let's take it from the top and do it carefully this time."

First they went around the house. Satsuki went clockwise and Tatsuo went counterclockwise.

Satsuki ran over to the pond on the far side of the garden. Mei often liked to take a stick and stir up the pollywogs and water beetles in the puddles of water that were all that was left of the pond. Maybe she would find a clue there.

"Daddy! Come look at this!" But as soon as she called to her father, Satsuki left the pond and went toward something else she had just spotted, like a dog on a scent.

"What is it? Did you find Mei?"

"No, but look over by the rocks next to the pond. Mei dropped her tote bag."

"Satsuki, what are you doing?" Tatsuo was puzzled to see Satsuki stopping again and again to pick something off the ground.

"Acorns. Remember? We found some the day we moved in. The soot sprites left them. There are lots of acorns on the ground here. See, now here's another one. Daddy, maybe Mei left them?"

As Satsuki was busily parting the grass, hunting for more acorns, Tatsuo spotted something on the ground a little farther away. He hurried over to Satsuki.

"Maybe she went that way. There's her hat. See? Over by the bushes."

A cranberry thicket ran along the edge of the garden between the yard and the Tsukamori Woods. Mei's yellow straw hat peeked out from beneath the leafy branches that bent toward the ground.

They ran to the hat lying on the ground and parted the branches anxiously. To their surprise, a path led away into the bushes, like a little tunnel enclosed by long branches.

"It looks like a secret trail, Daddy." Satsuki was certain the path would lead them to Mei.

The branches rustled as she parted them. She had to get down on her hands and knees to fit in the tunnel.

Where did it lead?

"Mei? Mei!"

The tunnel was enclosed by branches growing in all directions. As she moved down the passage, dry leaves and roots protruding from the ground made rustling and snapping sounds. The sun shone here and there through the leaves, dappling the path with little pools of light.

After what seemed like a long time, Satsuki saw a wider space like a circle and the edge of a skirt. It was Mei!

"There you are!"

Mei was lying on the ground.

Satsuki could feel her heart pounding and a sharp pain in her chest. Was she dead? Was she hurt?

As she ran, she prayed desperately that her sister would be all right. *Please let her be alive. Let her be okay. I'll never tease her again. She can play with Anne anytime she wants. She can bite me when I'm brushing her hair. I'll never get mad at her again, so please, please, please, let her be alive!*

In a few moments Satsuki was at Mei's side. Fearfully, she touched her shoulder.

"Mei?"

Satsuki shook her shoulder, hard.

"Mei! Mei!"

Mei groaned. She curled up in a ball. She was just sleeping! Satsuki felt a rush of relief that quickly changed to fury.

"Mei! Come on, wake up! What are you doing? We were so worried!" Satsuki shook her angrily. What had happened to her prayer?

"Mmm..." Mei's eyes opened a little and looked sleepily up at Satsuki. She murmured, "Totoro."

"Totoro?" Satsuki said, still angry. "What's that supposed to mean?"

Mei sat up, suddenly awake. She looked around quickly, surprised and puzzled. "Totoro? Where's Totoro?"

It was Satsuki's turn to be perplexed. Mei kept peering around anxiously, looking as if she had no idea how she had ended up in this hidden bower. She ran her fingers through the dirt as if she'd never seen dirt before. Now Satsuki was really worried.

"Here you are. Well, that's a relief. I brought your hat." Tatsuo crawled out of the tunnel and stood up under the green dome. He was wearing Mei's straw hat. As he took it off and held it out to her, his expression changed. "What's wrong, Mei?"

"Daddy, she keeps looking for something called Totoro. Isn't that right, Mei?"

Mei stood up and nodded.

"Totoro? Can you tell us what that is?" said Tatsuo gently. "You mean a troll, like in the fairy tales?"

Mei looked wide-eyed at her father and shook her head. She looked very serious.

"Not a troll. Totoro. That's what he said. He said Totoro."

"It talked to you?" Satsuki and Tatsuo exchanged surprised glances. They were both thinking Mei might have seen a dog or a cat. Even a raccoon wouldn't be a surprise this close to the woods. Whatever sort of animal it was, it was just an animal, and Mei had decided to call it Totoro. At least that made sense.

"Totoro can talk?" asked Satsuki. "Was it a person?"

"No!" Mei was adamant. "It was Totoro. He was sooo big!" Mei spread her arms wide, arched her back, and opened her mouth and eyes as wide as she could, as if Totoro was as big as the whole world. "All covered with fur. Soft and fluffy!"

Satsuki and Tatsuo gaped at her.

"I saw him! I even fell asleep on his tummy."

It had to have been a dream. Satsuki felt sure of it. Mei was just confusing a dream with the real world.

"But, Mei," Satsuki urged her, "what kind of an animal was it? Totoro's an animal, right?"

"I guess," Mei told her. "I don't know."

"Was it like a raccoon?"

"Mm-hm."

"Was it like a fox?"

"No."

"A cow?"

"No!"

"Was it like a tiger?"

"Oh, no."

"Was it a cat?"

"Maybe a little bit."

"How about a rabbit?"

"Sort of."

"A rabbit cat raccoon?" Satsuki cocked her head and smiled.

"That talks!" Mei stamped her foot. "Don't make fun of me! I saw him. I'm not fibbing. I saw little totoros too. And the big one told me his name. I just saw him."

"What? You saw little ones too?" Satsuki was flummoxed.

"Sure I did. Like this." Mei bent over and held her palm about knee high. "Two little totoros. They faded in and out."

Tatsuo, who had been listening without saying a word, finally spoke. "This is very interesting." He bent down with his hands on his knees and peered at Mei with a curious look. "Can you tell your father where you met Totoro?"

Mei answered excitedly. "At the pond. A little one. I chased him. He faded out. But I found him anyway. And another one."

Now Satsuki was curious too. "Listen, Mei. Was the little one a rabbit cat raccoon too?"

Mei stared up at the branches and tried to remember. "Not a rabbit. Not a bird. He had little eyes."

Tatsuo and Satsuki were even more confused. Mei was very earnest. "When he walked around"—she pointed to her tummy—"I could see the grass right through him."

"You could see through it?" asked Satsuki.

"Mm-hm."

Satsuki rolled her eyes. "That sounds like a ghost."

"No, it was a totoro. Not a ghost."

"You saw it by the pond, right?" asked Tatsuo. "What happened after that?"

"I found acorns," said Mei. Her voice grew stronger as she thought back. "The totoro dropped acorns on the ground, and I picked them up."

Satsuki took the acorns from her pocket and held them out to Mei. "I found some too."

"See? He was dropping them all over the place."

The acorns, at least, were real. Bright green, with little brown caps.

"I followed the trail of acorns to the tunnel," said Mei.

"What happened next? Where did the totoros go?"

"Inside the tree."

"What tree?"

"This one," said Mei and suddenly dashed to the other side of the clearing. The next moment she parted the branches and disappeared.

"More tunnels!" exclaimed Tatsuo.

Satsuki grinned and ran into the tunnel after Mei. Tatsuo was too big to go through very quickly. "Hey, wait for me!" he laughed, but Mei and Satsuki were already gone.

Mei ran through the leafy tunnel as fast as she could, with Satsuki close behind. The path sloped upward, then fell gradually.

"Here!" Mei shouted as she popped out of the thicket. Then Satsuki was right beside her. Mei froze and her mouth opened in surprise. "What...?"

Satsuki was just as surprised.

They were back in the garden!

They were standing at the entrance to the tunnel. They had come right back out the way they went in.

"How did that happen?" Satsuki said, completely confused. "It felt like we were going toward Tsukamori Woods."

"Before, I went to the laurel tree," said Mei.

"Through this tunnel? Are you sure?"

"Mm-hm."

"To the big laurel tree?"

"Mm-hm. That's where Totoro lives. Inside the tree."

Tatsuo finally caught up with them, snapping twigs and shaking the leaves as he shimmied out. "So this is where it comes out again. It's like a maze in there." He stood up, brushing the twigs and leaves off his face and shirt.

"But there was only one path," Satsuki said. "Are you sure it went to the woods, Mei?"

Mei ran back into the tunnel.

"Now hold on, Mei! Come back here!" shouted Tatsuo.

"Daddy, Mei says this tunnel leads to Totoro. She says Totoro lives inside the laurel tree." Satsuki supposed she'd better go after Mei again. They'd been through the tunnel once already and it wasn't as scary as before. Still, who knew what might happen? Maybe the tunnel would twist back on itself and steal Mei away from them this time.

But before Satsuki could follow her, Mei burst out of the tunnel with a rustling of leaves and a snapping of twigs, just behind where Tatsuo was standing.

"Oh! Oh!" Mei shouted in surprise, turning round and round to look at the garden and then back at the tunnel. She looked so astonished that Tatsuo and Satsuki couldn't help but laugh.

"It's true. I'm not fibbing!" Mei cried. "Don't laugh! Totoro was there. Inside the laurel. It's the truth."

Little by little, her little round eyes filled with tears and the corners of her mouth turned down.

Satsuki didn't know what to say. She looked up at her father. It *was* funny, after all.

"We're sorry, Mei. It's just...It's so unbelievable."

Was Totoro real? It would hardly do to take Mei's word for it, but Satsuki's hand closed around the acorns in her pocket.

"Mei," said Tatsuo solemnly, "I know very well you wouldn't tell a lie." He took her hand and looked up at the laurel. "Maybe what you met was the guardian of this forest. If you really did, it will bring you good luck. That's what Daddy thinks." As he spoke, Tatsuo looked up at the tree. His voice was filled with reverence. What a wonderful, spectacular tree it was!

"Now listen to me, both of you. Spirits that live in places like this won't come out and play whenever you want them to. The best way to get along with Totoro is to remember that." He smiled. "Remember what Mrs. Ogaki says? 'Leave the spirits be. Leave 'em be, and pay 'em your respects.'"

"Right," Satsuki said, recalling what Granny often told her. "If you don't, they'll move somewhere else."

"Is Totoro going to leave, Daddy?" asked Mei. Tears forgotten, she looked suddenly worried.

"Well you see, that's the point," said Tatsuo slowly, so Mei could understand. "As long as you don't try to look for him, I think Totoro will stay put. If you leave him alone, he won't move away."

Tatsuo picked Mei up with a "Ho!" and put her on his shoulders. "Shall we go for a walk?"

"Where?" Satsuki and Mei said together.

"The guardian of the woods was kind to Mei. We better go and give thanks. We moved in and haven't paid our respects yet, even though we're neighbors."

The light was gloomy among the chestnuts, beeches, and oak trees of Tsukamori Woods. Satsuki bounded up the stone steps to the old shrine at the foot of the giant laurel. The grounds around the little shrine were lonely with neglect. The stone water basin lay toppled on its side. The names of donors from generations past, inscribed on stone lanterns whose crowns lay fallen on the ground, were weathered away and hard to make out.

"Mei, you're getting heavy," Tatsuo said as he climbed the stairs after Satsuki.

"Look, Daddy! Isn't it beautiful?"

Satsuki stood at the base of the great tree gazing upward. From this close, the laurel looked almost supernatural. It would have taken forty or fifty children like Satsuki and Mei to encircle its huge trunk with hands joined. The surrounding trees nodded in the wind, endlessly bowing toward it in silent respect.

Rays of sunlight angled down, lighting up the trunks of some trees and leaving others in cool dimness. Satsuki couldn't begin to imagine how she might describe the laurel's size. Could a hundred carpenters working for a hundred years use all the wood in this great tree? Its branches seemed to hold up the sky, with enough space for all the birds in the woods to nest. It towered over her, moving and swaying in the wind, whispering endlessly without words.

*If the forest has a ruler, this must be where it lives*, thought Satsuki. *A ruler that wouldn't care whether or not you wanted to meet it. It would meet you when the time was right.*

The pale blue of the heavens hung far above the trees, but to Satsuki, the massive canopy of branches sighing high above her head seemed greater than the sky itself.

"Isn't it grand? Isn't it beautiful?" Tatsuo said as he stood beside her. "This tree has been here for centuries, watching the world change around it. Did I tell you two? This is the reason I fell in love with our house. So what if it's falling apart and people say it's haunted. That house and this tree need each other."

He stood looking up at the laurel and spoke to his daughters as grown-ups. "It attracted me like a magnet. A long time ago, people lived in harmony with the forest. Both were inseparable, like mother and child."

"Like Mommy and us?" asked Satsuki.

"That's right."

"Then," Satsuki said merrily, "is this tree in the hospital?"

"The hospital? I'm not so sure about that."

*Yasuko Kusakabe*
*Ward 5 South, Women's Sanatorium,*
*Shichikokuyama Hospital*
*Matsugo Shichikokuyama, Zawa County*

*Dear Mother,*
*How are you feeling? Everyone here is fine.*
*I have some big news, so get ready. I think*

*Mei met some kind of spirit. She drew you a picture. I'll send it with this letter.*

*Whatever she met, she says it's really huge. His (?) name is Totoro. Mei says she saw two others like him but lots smaller. She says she followed the little ones on a secret path to the big laurel in Tsukamori Woods and into a hole in the tree, and she fell and rolled down into a big room where Totoro was sleeping. She told us Totoro isn't scary at all.*

*I really envy her. I don't know if what she says is true, but since then I've been to the tree lots of times to pay my respects. Daddy says we can't meet Totoro whenever we want to. He says we shouldn't look for him. But still, wouldn't it be fun if I could meet him?*

*That's all for now.*

*If I meet Totoro, I'll be sure to tell him that you're looking forward to meeting him too.*

*I'll write again soon.*

*Satsuki*

## 5. The Rainy Day

Tatsuo had said he would find someone to help around the house, but no one came. Maybe Mother was right; perhaps they couldn't afford it. The three of them would just have to make do on their own.

At first, Satsuki had to run the mile to her new school without even having breakfast. She often missed the first bell because Tatsuo slept in. It was hard for him to get up after working all night to meet a translation deadline.

Finally, after being late to school once too often, Satsuki learned to get up early and make breakfast herself. Of course she packed her own lunch as well.

Granny Ogaki was astonished at how quickly Satsuki learned to heat the bath, light the fire, and cook over charcoal. Satsuki loved the smell of the burning wood, the colors in the flame, the glowing heat, and the way the wood crackled and threw sparks.

Cooking with the little charcoal stove was a challenge. The coals were either too hot or not hot enough, and different foods needed different amounts of heat.

When she lost track of time watching the fire for the bath, Satsuki found the rice burned black in the bottom of the pot. Even if she had soaked it for half a day before cooking it, once the rice was burned it took ages to scrape off.

If she stewed vegetables in soy sauce, the liquid was sure to come spitting out from under the lid of the pot. Startled, she would heap ashes on the coals to cool the grill and come back later to find that the fire had gone out completely.

Then there was fish. Grilling one side of the fish was easy, but then she had to flip it over, and it always seemed to fall through the grill onto the coals. Trying to pick it up with her fingers almost always meant getting burned. When she used the steel cooking chopsticks, the fish would slide around and she couldn't get a grip on it. Things got really exciting if she tried to stab it with the chopsticks. The fish would break apart and fall down between the coals, and the fat would send up white smoke and little spattering balls of flame.

And so, by trial and many errors, she learned to cook, and whether undercooked or burned Satsuki ate her failures without regret. Why be picky? She was managing breakfast by herself, and whatever she made tasted good because she'd made it. She ate a solid breakfast, packed herself a big lunch, and walked to school feeling like she owned the morning.

Granny Ogaki was Satsuki's stalwart ally. She always seemed to be "in the neighborhood," as she would say, to stop by and lend a hand. If not for Granny, Satsuki and Mei would have found each day much harder without their mother.

Perhaps because all of Granny's children and grandchildren were boys, she took special pleasure in looking after the two girls. They were overjoyed to see her, and she always brought them something from her kitchen.

Granny never seemed to worry what time it was. She got up with the sun and went home when it went down. She took things slow and easy, never hurrying at all. No matter how often Satsuki asked Granny to teach her something, Granny never complained, and no matter how often Satsuki made the same mistake, she never lost her patience.

"Now, now," she'd say with a chuckle, "watch the oil. Frying ain't the same as deep frying."

As time went on, one little problem after another was smoothed out. But there was one problem they couldn't solve. Sometimes Tatsuo had to be away all day, working at the university. So, what to do with Mei? At first Tatsuo and Satsuki were completely at a loss. Of course they couldn't leave her alone while Tatsuo was out and Satsuki was at school. Satsuki's classmate Miyoko was the only person outside the family that shy, retiring Mei felt at home with. But of course, when Satsuki was at school, Miyoko was there too. Asking a stranger to babysit Mei would be unfair. She would've been miserable.

The only solution was to rely on Granny to look after Mei on the days when Tatsuo was out and Satsuki was at school.

The evening before he would be away for the first time, Tatsuo made playful promises to Satsuki and Mei to boost their spirits.

"Mei, you have a tough day ahead tomorrow. Tomorrow night, you can stay up as late as you want."

"Great!"

"You can stay up all night while I work, if you feel like it."

"Really?"

"You don't even have to brush your teeth."

"Awesome!"

"Satsuki, what's the name of that magazine you like? Girl something?"

"*Girl's Club*," Satsuki said.

"Then I'll buy you a copy."

"Thanks, Daddy!"

"You've got a big day tomorrow too, so as a special bonus, you can read *Girl's Club* in the bath and I won't say a thing."

Satsuki laughed. She loved to read, even when she was taking a walk. Even in the bathtub! She would sit in the water holding the book with her left hand and turning the pages with her right. If her hand got wet, she turned the pages with her tongue. If the book was heavy, it sometimes fell in the water, and if Tatsuo caught her she never heard the end of it.

"Satsuki, go get a sheet of paper and a pencil," Tatsuo told her. "Let's discuss our to-do list for tomorrow. That way, whenever I have to go to work, you'll have a plan all ready."

_ *Get up (Everybody). Fold futons*
_ *Make breakfast (Daddy, Satsuki). Make box
   lunches (don't forget!)*
_ *Daddy leaves for the bus at 6:42*
_ *Satsuki and Mei leave at 7:50 for Granny's. Take
   change of clothes for Mei*

"Write 'Mei should put her crayons in her
bag,'" Mei said. Satsuki wrote it down.

_ *Mei — crayons in bag*
_ *Satsuki to school*
_ *After school, Satsuki picks up Mei*
_ *Afternoon snack in cupboard*
_ *Rice crackers in second drawer*
_ *Daddy home (5:15 bus)*
_ Girl's Club *for Satsuki*

"I'll pick up something for dinner," Tatsuo
said. "There's a butcher's shop behind the university that makes fantastic croquettes."

"Croquettes!" Mei and Satsuki said and
clapped their hands. How long had it been since
they'd eaten croquettes? They'd almost forgotten
what they tasted like.

_—Main dish: croquettes_
_—Make rice, miso soup_
_—Have dinner (Everybody)_

"Daddy, should I heat the bath before you come home?"

"No, don't start the fire till I get back. And let's make the rice for dinner in the morning. That way we can save time."

"I can do it after I get home, you know."

"But it's extra work."

Satsuki erased _Make rice, miso soup_. "Okay, that's it," she said. "Daddy? Can I call this to-do list 'Croquette Day'?"

The morning of Croquette Day was completely different from other mornings. Everyone got up before dawn and rushed to finish everything on the list.

After breakfast, Satsuki dressed Mei in her best one-piece dress. The dress had belonged to Mother when she was little. She had altered it for Satsuki, and Satsuki finally handed it down to Mei. When she wore it, Mei looked like a different girl. Maybe it was the bright red and green check pattern, but it made her look stylish and new.

"Mei, that dress is you," Tatsuo said.

"It used to be Mommy's," Mei said proudly, and put her hat on with a flourish.

Tatsuo was wearing his gray suit. "What do you think? Do I look like a professor?"

"Hmm…" Satsuki looked him up and down carefully. "It looks awfully wrinkled. Shouldn't we iron it?"

"It's wrinkled," Mei said.

"Who cares about a few wrinkles?" Tatsuo smiled. "The important thing is to wear it."

He peered at himself in Mother's dressing table mirror and moved his tie from side to side, trying to get it right.

"What are you doing, Daddy?" Mei said.

Tatsuo loosened his tie and pulled it off. "I don't like the way this looks. No necktie today."

Satsuki looked worried. "But, Daddy…men always wear ties when they go to work. Are you sure it's okay?"

"No problem. Archaeologists don't have to wear ties. Oh no, the time!" The clock in the living room chimed once, faintly. "It's 6:30. I have to go!"

He put on his white cap and said, "You two be good today." Then he shook hands solemnly with each of them. "If you start to worry, remember what I'm bringing home tonight."

They followed him to the entryway. He put his shoes on and picked up his briefcase. "All right, Satsuki, I'm leaving you in charge. Tell Mrs. Ogaki I'll drop by tonight to thank her. And don't forget to thank her yourself for helping us out." He threw open the sliding front door. "See you tonight. Be good!"

He left the door open and started off toward the road, glancing at his wristwatch. Then he was gone.

"See you tonight!" Satsuki called after him. She went back to the living room and looked at the clock. "I wonder if Daddy will catch the bus?"

"Why did he leave so soon?" Mei asked.

"Because it's really far from here to the university."

Satsuki decided not to worry about finishing the breakfast dishes. She could do them when she got home.

Now the hard part of the day began.

"I already wiped my face! I did!" Mei

complained as Satsuki wiped her face with a towel, hard enough to flatten her little nose.

"You can't go out with soy sauce on your chin," Satsuki told her. "You're going visiting today. You have to be neat."

*Now, ready, set, go!*

Satsuki locked the front door, and they walked down the path to the bridge, leaving the empty house behind them. The road was wet with dew. The little stream ran dark and twisting beside the road. The primrose blossoms gaped lazily. The pencil case in Satsuki's backpack rattled as she walked along. Matsugo Village lay wrapped in sleep. The air was filled with the smell of pennyroyal and pine needles.

Satsuki pretended to lag behind Mei, and Mei laughed with delight as she marched along the road. She held the bag Mother had made for her tightly under her shoulder as she pranced and skipped along.

Down the road, outside Kanta's house, Granny was waiting.

"Good morning, Granny!" Satsuki called out.

"Good morning. Welcome, welcome," Granny said and smiled. Mei held Satsuki's hand tight.

"Kanta's waiting for you. He wants you to

help him collect the eggs from the hens." Granny took Mei's other hand.

"Eggs?" Mei said, looking up at her.

"That's right. Shall we go? Kanta's waiting for you by the hen house."

"Okay."

"Better say goodbye to your sister."

"Okay." She let go of Satsuki's hand and waved. "Bye-bye," she said and let Granny guide her toward the house. "Can I pick some eggs too?"

"Of course you can," Granny said. She turned to look at Satsuki, nodding as if to say, You'd better go now. She looked up at the sky. It was bright blue with white clouds. "Looks like rain this afternoon. You'll need an umbrella."

"Thanks for your help," Satsuki said and bowed. Then she started back the way she had come.

Sawaida No. 2 Elementary School was about a mile to the east, past Satsuki's house and Tsukamori Woods. As she reached the footbridge again, Satsuki wondered if she should go in the house and get her umbrella. She was a little worried about what Granny had said.

"Satsuki, wait up!" Satsuki turned and saw

Miyoko running toward her along the shortcut between the rice paddies. "Wait for me. Let's go together," Miyoko called.

*Maybe I don't need that umbrella anyway*, Satsuki thought and waved at Miyoko.

The sky was deep blue and the clouds were very white. There were a lot of clouds, but the sun was shining. The weather was fine, Satsuki decided. It didn't look like rain at all. She waited for Miyoko to catch up.

"Good morning, Miyoko. We better get going!"


Sawaida No. 2 Elementary School was a big, cozy wooden building. Satsuki's last school had been close to a bustling shopping district. It was built of concrete and steel and must have had twice as many students as her new school. The atmosphere at Sawaida was much more relaxed as well.

The walk to school was also very different. Once Satsuki walked past the little lake that lay on the other side of Tsukamori Woods, there was nothing but rice paddies all the way. Just beyond the lake, the railroad ran along a high embankment extending north and south, with a bridge where the tracks ran above the road. Unless the train was passing by, the only sounds were the voices of children on their way to school, the wind, and the birds calling.

Satsuki was astonished when she learned that the school custodian, Mr. Karaki, and his wife lived in the school building. Down the wide hall just inside the front door and to the left was the custodian's office, but everyone called it the Karaki house. If you dropped by after class and peeked in the open doorway, you were likely to see Mr. and Mrs. Karaki drinking tea and eating sweets. One day, when Satsuki went there to borrow a bucket, old Mr. Karaki let her "steal" one of his sweet potato pastries.

Everything was different from her old school.

Fourth period was composition. Children in Japan take a long time to learn all the characters needed to write the language. But Satsuki loved to read, and when it came to practicing her Chinese characters or writing an essay she was like a magician compared to the other students, here and at her last school. She finished her in-class assignments faster than anyone and rarely made mistakes. She had a natural ability for writing, almost like the talent a monkey has for climbing trees.

Satsuki thought arithmetic was very boring, but she never tired of composition class. Today she finished her character drill before the others and was enjoying looking out the window. Her teacher, Reiko Moriyama, walked around the classroom checking the students' progress.

Miss Moriyama had recently graduated from college and was new to teaching. Sometimes, when the students were especially noisy, she'd say, "Oh dear, what shall I do? I'm so sad I think I'm going to cry." Sometimes she really did look like she was going to cry. But usually she was very cheerful. Miss Moriyama was kind and worked quite hard to teach her students.

Satsuki noticed Miss Moriyama looking out the window and up at the sky with a worried expression. It was getting a bit cloudy.

Out in the playground between the gate and the school building, the sixth graders had divided up into a red team and a white team and were running relay races. *Looks like fun*, thought Satsuki. She loved to run. She'd competed on the track team at her last school, but running was something the kids here seemed to be especially good at. Satsuki wasn't sure she was fast enough to compete with them.

While she daydreamed, her eyes wandered toward the front gate.

"Hmm?"

No, it couldn't be. She squinted to make out something just outside the pair of stone pillars that marked the entrance to the schoolyard. Just beyond them she could see something red and green.

*Mei?*

She was about to dismiss the thought when Granny Ogaki stepped out from behind a pillar. It was Granny and Mei, all right. What was wrong? Had Mei thrown a tantrum? Leaving her with Granny didn't seem to have worked out after all.

*What should I do?* Satsuki thought. Her heart was pounding with embarrassment. For a few moments, all she could do was sit there frozen. She was a new student, and after being late more often than most, she already stuck out. Now here was Mei.

Satsuki always tried to be organized and efficient like her mother. It upset her when things didn't go according to plan. She might seem confident and fearless to others, but inside she was a worry-wart. She was sensitive. She lost her temper easily and panicked just as easily.

Mei and Granny just stood there, outside the gate. Satsuki gave up and raised her hand. "Miss Moriyama?" she said, trying not to attract attention.

"Yes, Satsuki, just a few minutes more. We're almost finished."

"No, it's not that. My sister is here."

"What?"

"My little sister. She's out by the gate." Satsuki pointed.

A little murmur arose from the class. The other children were all ears now. Satsuki stammered, "She, she was supposed to spend the day at Kanta's house, but…"

A few students made mock exclamations of surprise, as if Satsuki and Kanta had a secret that had just been revealed. This made everyone laugh. Kanta stared straight ahead, his face grim.

"All right, everyone," Miss Moriyama said. "Satsuki's mother is in the hospital, remember? She needs our support." She opened the window and looked toward the gate again. "Well, we can't just let them stand there. Is your father out today, Satsuki?"

"Yes."

"Kanta, your grandmother's here."

This brought another murmur of mock surprise from the class. Everyone was enjoying this welcome bit of unexpected entertainment. It was fun for everyone except the two people concerned. Kanta was dying of embarrassment. Only if his mother had been standing out there would things have been worse.

"Satsuki?" Miss Moriyama said.

"Yes, Teacher."

"Go to the gate and find out what's the matter."

"Yes, Teacher."

"Teacher! Teacher!" Hands went up all over the classroom. "Can I go too? I want to see the little girl." Several students were talking at once. "Please, can I go?" "The kids by the window get to see everything. It's not fair!" "I want to go!" "Let me go too!" The classroom was in an uproar. Satsuki couldn't wait anymore. She got up and ran out to the entrance, where her outdoor shoes were waiting.

"All right, everyone," Miss Moriyama said, rather irritated. "You can look, but please be quiet. Otherwise I'm going to close the curtains."

Satsuki ran right through the middle of the relay race to the gate. It was sultry and hot. Granny saw Satsuki coming toward them and waved. She looked relieved.

"Mei said she wanted to go to the school," Granny explained apologetically. Mei was staring down at her shoes. "She wouldn't take no for an answer."

"There, you see?" Granny said to Mei. "Your sister's right here. Say hello to her, then be a good girl and let Granny take you back."

As soon as she said this, Mei stretched out her arms and, still looking down, hugged Satsuki's legs.

"Let's go, Mei," said Granny gently. "Satsuki has lessons to finish. She'll be along soon." Mei didn't answer. Granny stroked Mei's hair and shook her head helplessly. "She was such a good girl today."

Granny and Satsuki both knew that trying to pry Mei away from her sister would be futile, but they didn't know what else to do.

"Mei, I can't come with you. School's not over yet," Satsuki said.

Mei's eyes filled with tears that ran down her cheeks. She hugged Satsuki tighter and pushed her toward the school. Satsuki had had enough. She pulled away from Mei.

Mei began to cry, a loud wail that came from deep inside. Some of the sixth graders turned to stare at her.

"Don't cry, Mei. Please don't cry. Everyone's looking," Satsuki said, now thoroughly embarrassed again. Mei started crying even harder. It was time to give up. Satsuki looked tiredly at Granny Ogaki. "I'll tell the teacher I have to leave early." She looked down at Mei again. "Mei, please stop crying. Let's go. Granny, thanks for helping us again today. I'll take Mei home."

"I'm sorry I couldn't do more," Granny said.

"All right, Mei. Come on, I have to get my backpack." Satsuki dried her tears with the handkerchief she kept in her skirt pocket. "Stop crying, now. We have to drop by my classroom."

"I'll be going, then," Granny said. "I'm sorry you have to do this." And she turned and walked away.

Satsuki walked dejectedly back toward her classroom with Mei in tow. *You're not the only one who feels like crying, Mei!*

Satsuki glanced at her classroom windows. "Oh, no..."

Everyone in class was crowded at the windows, watching Satsuki and Mei expectantly. She could hear them laughing and talking, commenting on how cute Mei was and wondering out loud what would happen next. Satsuki felt miserable.

When she stood in the classroom door with Mei, there was a huge commotion as some children scrambled to take their seats and others tried to get a closer look at Mei. There was a thunder of trampling of feet and scraping chairs.

"Why Satsuki, your little sister is adorable," Miss Moriyama exclaimed. "Now back to your seats, everyone. Right this minute!"

Everyone sat down, but they kept craning their necks to get a look at Mei. Satsuki walked to the front of the class. On the wall behind her, the results of yesterday's Chinese character drill had been posted—thirty-four examples of the phrase "A generous heart," one by each student.

Finally, when everyone had settled down, Miss Moriyama studied Mei again and said, "You are without a doubt a very, very cute little girl."

*Cute?* Satsuki winced. After what Mei had done to her, she felt like grinding her teeth. "Miss

Moriyama, can I have permission to leave early?"

"Why?" the whole class said in unison.

"Yes, why?" Miss Moriyama said.

"Well, obviously…" Satsuki started to say. Hands shot up again.

"Teacher!" "Teacher!"

"All right. Junko?" Miss Moriyama pointed to Junko Naoi. She stood up, ramrod straight.

"Why don't we let Satsuki's sister study with us?"

"Teacher!" "Teacher!"

Miss Moriyama pointed to another student. "Yukio?"

Yukio Iwata stood up. "I don't think it's fair to make them stay at home alone," he said.

"Well, it's an interesting idea," Miss Moriyama said pensively, gazing at Mei.

Miyoko stood up, though she hadn't been called on. "We'll all take care of her, Miss Moriyama. You don't have to worry."

"Teacher!" Kohei Iida, the class president, raised his hand. "We could bring a chair from the music room. Mei could sit next to Satsuki."

"Well, I guess that would be the best thing to do," Miss Moriyama said. Everyone started clapping and cheering.

"Big sister?"

"What?" Satsuki was startled at being called "big sister" by Miss Moriyama.

"Please bring a chair from the music room—oh, that's right, Miss Kusakabe can't be separated from her big sister."

Satsuki couldn't believe it. Miss Moriyama was referring to Mei as "Miss Kusakabe."

"Well then," Miss Moriyama said, "Masaé."

"Yes, Miss Moriyama."

"Please bring a chair from the music room for Miss Kusakabe."

"All right." A murmur of envy rose from the students. Going to get a chair was a grand assignment. Masaé left for the music room happily.

"Miss Kusakabe, would you like to study with us? You'll have to study quietly. Can you do that?"

Mei's eyes sparkled. "Yes, Teacher!" Everyone laughed and clapped some more. Satsuki was too embarrassed to join in. Kanta thought the whole situation was getting more embarrassing for him too, and he kept his grim face.

"Now then, little Miss Kusakabe, what is your first name?" Miss Moriyama asked.

"Mei."

"Mei, your chair is here, so please sit down next to your sister." Satsuki went to her seat. Mei followed in high spirits and sat down.

From then until the end of the school day, Mei was a member of the class. Miss Moriyama gave her paper to draw on. She drew all kinds of pictures. Satsuki's face. Totoro. Acorns shaped like apples.

"You better be quiet," Satsuki warned her, when Mei started talking to the pictures she was drawing.

"I am being quiet," Mei said earnestly. "I'm being a good girl."

After fourth period, it was time for lunch. The girls sitting near Mei competed to share something nice with her from their lunches. There was so much food that Miss Moriyama had to supervise. She let Mei use the upturned lid of her own lacquerware lunch box as a plate and placed little morsels on it as long as Mei had an appetite. Rice. A bit of omelet. Stewed vegetables.

"No croquettes," said Mei.

"Really? Don't you like them?" Miss Moriyama was surprised. Her chopsticks hovered over the lid of the lunch box with a bit of croquette from Satsuki's classmate Kazuko.

"I like them. Daddy's bringing us croquettes for dinner," Mei said, a bit self-importantly. "So I don't need one now."

"That makes sense." Miss Moriyama put the croquette back in Kazuko's lunch box.

Satsuki felt sorry for Kazuko. Mei had embarrassed her again.

All through lunch, everyone competed to be nice to Mei. After she finished eating, she sat drawing quietly and didn't fuss or fret at all. Still, when the afternoon bell rang and Satsuki walked through the gate with Mei, she felt a surge of relief that things were finally getting back on track.

It was hot. They were both sweating. Satsuki had a hard time keeping hold of Mei's hand. Soon after they left the school, she could see a bank of rain clouds coming toward them. Far off, the landscape was dark under the lowering clouds. It was already raining there.

Very soon it began to rain where they were. A few drops at first, but big ones, darkening the dust in the road.

"Come on, Mei, we better run!" Satsuki said as she took off. Mei ran as hard as she could. Raindrops splashed down on them. A grove of bamboo by the roadside swayed as the rain pattered against its slender leaves. A flock of birds rose from the grove and flew away to the west, calling loudly. Farmers in the fields wiped the water from their faces. The rain drummed softly on the broad leaves of cucumber and taro plants along the road. The taro leaves were big enough to make an umbrella for a little girl or a hiding place from the rain. But the fields belonged to the farmers.

*Splash!* Mei tripped and went sprawling in the mud.

Satsuki had run a bit ahead. She ran back and helped Mei stand up. She was a sight to behold, muddy from head to toe.

Without Mei to look after, Satsuki would probably have enjoyed skipping home in the rain. Even if she'd had an umbrella, she might not have used it. But she could hardly expect her tiny sister to run home in the rain like a bedraggled mouse. Satsuki wondered why she hadn't just gone back to the school to get an umbrella when it started to rain. And this morning she'd had a chance to get one from home and didn't bother. Now here they were. Satsuki wondered why she hadn't been a little more careful. She wasn't the only one getting wet. She was getting very irritated with herself.

As they trudged along, the dim line of the railway embankment finally came into view. A few dozen yards before the road passed under the tracks, an old statue of Jizo stood watch by the roadside, sheltered by a little peaked roof. The girls ran under it to get a respite from the rain.

"I'm sorry I forgot to get an umbrella," Satsuki said as she wiped the mud off Mei's cheeks with her handkerchief.

"It's okay." Mei was calm. "I fell down, but I didn't cry."

"You're a brave girl." Satsuki peered out at the sky from under the little shelter. The rain was coming down harder. Was it ever going to stop? "Looks like we're stuck here, Mei."

A commuter train rumbled across the bridge above the road. Satsuki wondered if the passengers were carrying umbrellas. Daddy hadn't taken an umbrella this morning, just his cap and briefcase.

The paddies lay emerald green in the sheeting rain. The rice plants were so green it almost made you want to sneeze. The long, slender seedlings didn't move at all as the rain ran down them.

*You love the rain, don't you?* Satsuki thought as she gazed at the paddies. A scarecrow in worn old clothes and a straw hat was getting a good soaking. Satsuki wondered if the scarecrow would mind lending her his hat.

Kanta walked right past them, carrying an umbrella with a broken rib.

He glanced at Satsuki and Mei. For a moment he looked slightly confused, but he didn't stop. He just walked on down the road.

Satsuki sighed. The rain came sluicing down Jizo's battered old roof. Mei put a toe out into the little stream running down the road and watched the water flow around it.

Maybe they should make a run for home?

*This isn't going to stop anytime soon. Maybe I should go home and bring back an umbrella*, Satsuki thought, but she shook her head. She couldn't leave Mei here all by herself. She was so cute that someone was sure to come along and kidnap her.

A pair of wooden clogs came pounding toward them. Satsuki leaned out and looked down the road. It was Kanta. He ran up and held his umbrella out to her stiffly, at arm's length.

"Take it!"

Satsuki was so surprised, she did just what he told her. As soon as she took the umbrella, Kanta was off down the road with his backpack over his head, weaving and bounding over the puddles like a young colt. He ran under the bridge and disappeared in the rain.

## 6. The Bus Stop at Inari Shrine

Once the girls had gotten home, dried themselves off, combed their hair, and changed into clean clothes, they felt fresh and energetic. Now they could spend the rest of the day looking forward to Tatsuo's return. Today was a special day. They felt like laughing and running around.

How should they spend the rest of the afternoon?

Satsuki looked at the clock. It was a little past two thirty. It wouldn't be long until Tatsuo was home. She wanted to get everything ready before he arrived.

*This is great. Thanks, you two!*

Satsuki giggled happily, picturing how her father would smile when he saw how busy they'd been. She felt like she'd already done something good.

"Mei! Mei! Come in the living room."

Mei came running in, clutching her tote bag. "It's all dirty."

"It got mud on it when you fell down. Give it to me. I'll wash it for you," Satsuki said.

Good idea! They could wash their muddy clothes and do the rest of the laundry at the same time.

"Mei, get all the wet clothes. We'll wash them right now."

"Next to the tub?"

"That's right."

Satsuki went into the kitchen and attached the long tin pipe that led from the pump to the bathtub. She went into the bath, took the cover off the bathtub, went back into the kitchen, and worked the squeaky pump handle up and down. She heard water gurgling down the pipe into the tub.

Mei came down the hall with a bundle of dripping clothes, leaving a trail of water on the wooden floor. She held them out to Satsuki. "Here."

"Put everything in the washbasin."

"What do I do?" Mei said.

"Well, let's see. You can put water from the tub in the washbasin."

"Okay. I like that."

While they did the laundry they got wet all over again, so they took their clothes off and washed them along with everything else. Then they ran to

Mommy's room and changed into dry clothes. They combed their hair again and felt brand new.

"That takes care of the laundry. Let's have a snack," Satsuki said.

As they ate their snack, Satsuki looked at the to-do list. She took a pencil and drew a line through the things they had already finished.

"There's four more left," she said.

_Daddy home (5:15 bus)
_Girl's Club *for Satsuki*
_Main dish: croquettes
_Have dinner (Everybody)

Satsuki looked out at the garden. "It sure is raining hard."

"I know," Mei said.

The pond was filling with water. Tsukamori Woods looked blurry in the rain. The woodpile was soaked. The only sound they could hear was the rain on the roof.

Satsuki took the plates and cups into the kitchen and washed them in the sink. What next? She decided to get a head start on dinner. She opened the cupboard, looking for the tea tin that held the dried shrimp.

"Come out, come out, wherever you are…"

Satsuki found the tin, filled the pot with water from the pump, put it on the stove, and added shrimp to the water. "Five big ones, minus the heads."

Tatsuo had told her not to start the fire, but by soaking the shrimp now she could make miso soup in no time.

"Mei, put the chopsticks out. Teacups too."

They wiped the dining table and set out the plates, bowls, chopsticks, and teacups.

"Shall we lay out the futons?" Satsuki said. "Then when Daddy gets back, we won't have to do it."

"Mm-hmm." Mei nodded.

They ran into Mommy's room and laid out the futons. Mei ran around on the soft futons, laughing and doing somersaults. She dived into her futon. "Let's take a nap!"

The clock in the living room chimed once. It was four thirty.

Satsuki was beginning to worry about Tatsuo's umbrella. If she didn't take it to him at the bus stop, he'd be very wet by the time he got home. Then there was Kanta's umbrella. She'd better drop that off at the Ogakis' on the way to the bus stop.

"Listen, Mei. I want to take Daddy his umbrella. Would you like to take a nap while I'm gone?" That way, Satsuki could run to the bus stop just before the bus came. But Mei jumped up from her futon.

"I'm going too!"

"It's still raining. And the bus stop is pretty far."

"I'm going!"

"But you haven't had a nap today," Satsuki said. "Why don't you wait here in your futon?"

"Don't want to."

"You can play with Anne."

"Really?"

"I'll even let you change her clothes."

"Okay."

"So you'll wait here?"

"No!"

Satsuki gave up. "Then we better get you ready."

In her galoshes and hooded raincoat, Mei didn't need an umbrella. Satsuki put on her long rubber boots and took three umbrellas: her pink one, Tatsuo's big black one, and the one she borrowed from Kanta. Together they left the house again.

The path to the footbridge was slippery and wet. The stream was so swollen with muddy water that it could barely pass beneath the bridge. The wildflowers along its banks were half submerged. The paddies on the other side of the road were brimming. The footpaths between the fields glistened in the dim light of late afternoon.

The road was deserted. Satsuki and Mei set off toward the village.

Kanta's house was almost exactly halfway to the bus stop. Satsuki walked slowly so Mei didn't have to run.

"We're going to stop by Kanta's house," Satsuki told her. "If you see Granny, you'd better apologize for today."

Mei didn't answer.

"You don't want her to think you don't like her," Satsuki added.

No answer.

"Tell her you're sorry."

"No." Mei shook her head and looked down at the road. "I don't want to."

*If you're going to be so stubborn, Miss Moriyama won't let you come to school ever again,* Satsuki almost said, but she let it go. This wasn't the time or the place to upset Mei.

Satsuki opened the sliding door that opened onto the hard-packed floor of the Ogakis' big entryway. Luckily it was Kanta's mother who came out to greet them.

"What are you doing out in this rain?" She was surprised to see them. It was dinnertime. Satsuki could smell dried sardines grilling.

"Is something the matter?" Kanta's mother asked. "You'd better come in and join us for dinner."

The paper-covered lattice door to the living room rattled open. Kanta's little brother Shota peeked out. When he saw the two girls he slammed the door shut.

"Quit fooling around and finish your dinner, blockhead." It was Kanta's voice. Satsuki heard laughter. The radio was playing. Dishes rattled.

"Quiet down in there," Kanta's mother yelled through the doors.

Satsuki held out the umbrella. "I borrowed this from Kanta today. Thank you very much."

"I hope you'll excuse the noise," Kanta's mother said. "I've got four men in the house and it's always like this."

"It's all right, we're just stopping by. We got caught in the rain on the way back from school.

Kanta lent us his umbrella. He must've gotten soaked." She gave Kanta's mother the umbrella.

"Oh no," she said, looking at the umbrella. "Is this what Kanta's been taking to school? It's broken. I'm sorry you had to use this."

"No, it really helped. I had Mei with me. I'm glad he let us use it."

"Kanta!" his mother yelled again. "Satsuki's here." Satsuki heard running and roughhousing beyond the doors.

"Kanta, Mom wants you!" Shota yelled. Satsuki grabbed Mei's hand.

"I'm sorry. We've got to go. My father is on the five-fifteen bus. We're meeting him at the bus stop. He needs his umbrella."

"Give me five seconds." Kanta's mother went inside and returned with a handful of sugar candies wrapped in paper. She presented the candy to Mei.

"Thank you, Mrs. Ogaki. See you again," Satsuki said. The house was so busy that she felt almost relieved to be going.

Satsuki and Mei sucked on the candies as they walked in silence to the bus stop. Their own house was isolated, but as they got closer to the bus stop and the edge of the village, the houses were closer together. Light shone faintly from farm-house windows.

"Granny wasn't home," Mei said. "Maybe she was feeding Matsan."

"Matsu-san" was the Ogakis' cow.

"I helped her feed Matsan," Mei said.

"That must've been fun."

"There was lots of flies."

Shinmei Inari Shrine, dedicated to the fox god Inari, was just behind the bus stop in a grove of zelkova trees. By the time the girls turned the corner to the bus stop, the candy was gone, but they could already hear the bus approaching. Headlights shone out of the deepening gloom. Wipers swept back and forth across the big wind-shield. The brakes squealed on the hard-packed dirt road as the bus stopped in front of the pole that marked the stop. The round sign on the pole said INARI SHRINE.

As soon as the bus stopped, the door opened. A man and a woman got off, and that was all. Tatsuo wasn't on the bus!

"Are you getting on?" The lady conductor leaned out the door. Satsuki shook her head. "All right!" the conductor said to the driver. The door closed and the bus started up again.

"Where's Daddy?" Mei said.

Satsuki stared tight-lipped at the bus as it drove away. The people inside looked snug and dry.

What to do?

"He must've missed the bus, Mei." The next bus would not be along for forty minutes.

"Isn't Daddy coming home?" Mei said.

"Of course he is. Don't talk nonsense."

Satsuki wished Mei had stayed home. Then it would've been easy to run home, wait, and come back.

"I guess we're stuck again, Mei." Then, to humor her sister, Satsuki added, "Marooned at the ends of the earth."

Maybe they should go home? Satsuki assumed that Tatsuo would carry Mei back on his shoulders. Making her walk home didn't seem like such a good idea. She'd already had enough walking for one day.

"What do you want to do, Mei? Do you want to stay here?"

"Mm-hmm." Mei was walking aimlessly around the bus stop. She stood in a puddle to see how deep it was. Exploring. She didn't seem interested in leaving.

"Wouldn't you rather go home?"

"Nope."

"The next bus won't be here for a long time. Are you sure?"

"I'm okay."

Mei peeked down the short flagstone path leading to the shrine. A faded red flag with the characters INARI THE GREAT hung next to the little shrine, which wasn't much taller than Satsuki. Mei toddled up to it.

"It's full of foxes!" she called.

Curious, Satsuki came to see for herself. She peered into the dimness and saw dozens of white ceramic fox figurines of different sizes. Some had open red mouths.

"It looks spooky," Satsuki said.

Mei played at ducking between the trunks of the huge zelkova trees that surrounded the shrine. The stately grove was a riot of lush, early-summer foliage. Framed by the deep green of new leaves, the dilapidated little shrine with its torn, sun-bleached flag, and even the solitary bus stop with its round sign and flaking paint, seemed cheerful and full of life.

Satsuki walked back to the pole. Its base was a block of concrete. "All right, we're going to wait," she called to Mei. She hung Tatsuo's umbrella on the little metal plate that was attached to the pole, with the bus schedule behind a cracked sheet of plastic. Then she ducked beneath the branches of a tall zelkova to get some shelter from the rain.

Yes, it was better to wait. It was too late to go home now.

Satsuki's thoughts wandered as she gazed off down the road. In the Terashima house, in the eight-mat room on the second floor that served as Yasuko's sickroom, she could be with her mother whenever she wanted. Satsuki could still see the big can of white powder and the transparent leaves of starch paper that her mother would wrap the medicine in to make it easier to swallow. She remembered how Yasuko would walk quickly past the chest of drawers in the six-mat room on her way to the platform outside where they always hung the laundry.

The closets.

Satsuki loved to jump down onto the tatami from the middle shelf of a closet. Yasuko would fold her arms, nod, and say, "Splendid! You're such a big girl now."

Aunt Kyoko would yell up the stairs. "Stop making such a racket!"

Then they were in trouble. What did Mother

always say? "I'm so sorry, Kyoko. It was an accident." And she and Satsuki would cover their mouths and giggle for the longest time. Mei hadn't been born yet, and Satsuki was still very small.

Their new house was close to the hospital, but Mother had never lived there with them. Without Tatsuo around, the house felt big and empty.

Satsuki walked to the bus stop. She took a loop of string from her pocket and started playing cat's cradle. Mei amused herself with the puddles along the road, kicking up splashes with the toe of her galoshes. She was being just as patient as her sister.

Still, it seemed the more they waited, the more slowly time passed.

The rain never let up.

A solitary streetlamp switched on. Its yellow bulb cast a faint pool of warm light next to the bus stop. Night had come.

Someone rode past on a bicycle. They saw the headlamp before they could see the bicycle squeaking and creaking up the road. Mei clutched Satsuki's skirt and watched warily as the hooded rider pedaled by, dripping in the rain.

Standing there with the darkness around her, Satsuki felt a little like a ghost. She imagined what it would be like to follow the man on the bicycle in the rain, the way a ghost would. She held her hands by her sides like a corpse and stared balefully after the bicyclist. But she stopped right away. It was too silly.

The minutes dragged. The water dripping from the branches sounded like clocks ticking. Satsuki looked up at the round sign.

AZUMA RAILROAD BUS LINE

FOR MAEZAWA

FOX GROVE

How many times had she read that sign?
When? When? When?
When was the bus coming?
"Where's the bus?" Mei said.
"It's not here yet," Satsuki said.
The night was inky beyond the glow of the streetlamp. They should've gone home with somebody from the bus. The man had turned the corner toward Satsuki's house. There was a shortcut through the grove to the village, but it was so dark now that Satsuki couldn't even see it. They really were marooned, marooned in a soft pool of yellow light.

The girls stood silently. Waiting. *We never should've come*, Satsuki thought. *We'd be home right now, playing on the futons.*

Mei kicked a puddle, staggered, and almost fell in the water. For the first time, Satsuki noticed how sleepy Mei was. Her eyelids drooped. She dragged them open and they shut again. Her eyes were staying shut longer and longer. She was falling asleep on her feet.

"Mei?" Satsuki grabbed her hand and shook it. Mei didn't answer. "You can't sleep here." Something had to be done right away.

"Do you want to walk to Granny's? Say something, Mei."

Mei hung her head sleepily and didn't answer. "It's not far," Satsuki said.

Why couldn't the bus just *come*? Satsuki squinted down the road till her eyes hurt.

"All right, sleepyhead," Satsuki sighed. "Come on." She squatted down with her back to Mei. "Hop on." Mei would be safer on her back. Otherwise she'd probably fall flat into a puddle.

Mei was practically asleep. She staggered toward Satsuki and put her arms around her sister's neck. Satsuki put her arms under Mei's legs and hoisted her onto her back. The umbrella slipped to one side. Big drops of water fell on their faces and necks.

Little Mei was so exhausted that she didn't notice. Satsuki could tell by her breathing that she was already sound asleep.

Satsuki leaned forward and stared at the puddle beneath her rubber boots. She had to stay in that position or Mei would slide off. She balanced the handle of the umbrella on her shoulder.

Tatsuo was right. Mei was getting heavy. Satsuki tried to keep her mind on the thought that the bus would be here soon.

*Drip, drip, drip...*

The rain kept falling, but the really big drops were coming from the branches above. The leaves rustled and sighed in the rain like a giant breathing softly. Now and then a bicycle would pass, tires hissing through the puddles. Satsuki always hoped it might be the bus, but it never was. And then the road would be empty again, and there was no sound except the rain and the murmuring leaves.

A gust of wind came through the grove and struck Satsuki from behind. It was a big puff of air, warm and dry.

She stood bent over like a statue, balancing Mei on her back and the umbrella over her shoulder. The darkness behind her seemed to writhe and squirm, as if something were passing through the trees. But it wasn't the wind. Then she heard a sound.

Footsteps.

Sodden leaves squished as heavy feet pressed against the earth. Shuffling steps crossed the stone path and splashed in the puddles. Slowly, slowly, the steps came toward them.

Satsuki listened hard. Behind the footsteps she could hear something dragging through the leaves.

A breath of air nudged her umbrella. The steps came beside her and stopped.

Someone was standing next to her. There was a scent in the air like nothing Satsuki had ever smelled before. Like dried grass, but sharper and heavier. She smelled straw and mugwort, lizard tail and mint, clover and daisies, all mixed up in a mysterious, pungent scent that cut through the smells of the rain and the mud and the trees.

The stranger just stood there. He didn't make a sound.

Satsuki wanted to see who it was, but with Mei on her back and the umbrella balanced on her shoulder, she couldn't look up. All she could see was the ground next to her feet.

She saw two huge legs. They were not human. Her heart started pounding.

Five long, curved claws gripped the ground, half hidden by downy, gray-violet fur. The legs were stout and short, and a paunch reached between the legs all the way to the ground. There was a long, thick tail.

Satsuki was terrified. She cowered under the umbrella. What was it?

Maybe it would pounce on her if she moved? The thought made her scalp crawl.

Moments ago she'd been ready to cry because Mei was so heavy. Now she was so surprised, she almost forgot Mei was there.

She waited. Nothing happened.

Very, very slowly, she lifted the edge of the umbrella. Next to her was an arm. It was heavy and broad, like the wing of a giant owl, and it ended in another set of long, curved claws.

The creature was scratching itself lazily.

The rain splashed and bounced off its gray fur.

As Satsuki gasped with surprise, she straightened up. Mei started to slip. Satsuki quickly heaved her back into place, but as she did, the umbrella fell to the ground.

That was when she saw the creature clearly for the first time.

She was so alarmed that she practically dropped her sister. She stood Mei roughly on her feet and shielded her with her arms. Then she grabbed the umbrella and hid them both beneath it. Mei rested her head against her sister's leg. She was asleep standing up.

The creature was huge. Long, serrated ears stood straight up from the top of its head like thistles. They looked so impressive, so alert and sensitive, that Satsuki was sure the creature could hear the slightest sound with those ears, maybe even think with them.

A big lotus leaf covered the creature's head between its ears like a rain hat. Big drops of water fell on the leaf with a popping sound and rolled off onto the creature's nose, which reminded Satsuki of a raccoon's. With each drop that fell on its nose, the creature twitched its long, stiff whiskers.

A creature like a raccoon, a rabbit, an owl, a cat...

Except for the lotus leaf on its head, the creature stood unprotected and seemingly oblivious to the rain. It gazed fixedly ahead, eyes wide open.

It wasn't acting dangerous. *Maybe we'll be okay,* thought Satsuki.

*Wait. Is this Totoro? Is this what Mei saw?*

*But what should I do? If I move or say something...what happens then?*

*What if this is the ruler of the forest, like Granny said?*

*Maybe it'll just go away. Or maybe it's an evil spirit. What if it comes after us with those claws?*

Satsuki didn't want the creature to go, and she didn't want it to pounce on her either. But there was something she had to ask it, something she had to know. She held Mei tightly, slowly tipped the umbrella back and looked up.

"Uhm...are you...are you Totoro?"

Almost imperceptibly the creature cocked its head, as if to say, Mm? Its ears swiveled in Satsuki's direction, so she knew it could hear her, though she'd barely spoken above a whisper. Its gaze wandered slowly over and down onto her. And then, with the faintest of smiles, it answered softly.

Its voice was deep but musical, like a reed flute played by the wind. The sound rose into the night and was lost in the rustling of the zelkova leaves. Was it some kind of call? It might have been the groan a gigantic tree trunk makes in the wind.

"You're Totoro," Satsuki declared.

This had to be Totoro. He had looked at her and said yes—this huge, bushy, gray hodgepodge of raccoon, owl, and bear.

"It *is* you! You're really Totoro!"

*I did it!* Satsuki was overjoyed. *I finally met Totoro!*

The rain bent the leaves. The leaves gathered the rain and poured it down on Totoro. The droplets sparkled in the light from the lamp as they flowed over his downy fur. Rain from the sky sluiced over his huge body in little waves.

Satsuki took Tatsuo's black umbrella from where she'd hung it on the sign. She popped it open and held it out to Totoro.

"Here."

Totoro's eyes widened with surprise. His ears twitched. He gazed in puzzlement at the umbrella.

"It's for the rain. Take it."

Totoro looked completely bewildered. Finally he took the handle of the umbrella gently between two long claws, like tweezers. Satsuki held her umbrella high over her head.

"Hold it like this. That way you won't get wet."

Totoro turned the umbrella this way and that, perplexed. He looked at Satsuki, then back at the umbrella.

*Something is happening*, Satsuki thought. Some mysterious intuition told her not to say more, but just to listen.

Suddenly Totoro whisked the umbrella up over his head and held it there. He gazed straight ahead again. The umbrella was just big enough to keep his huge head out of the rain.

The rain kept falling, falling, falling....

The sound of rain was everywhere.

It plopped in the mud and splashed in the puddles, slithered down the branches and tinkled from the leaf tips, a symphony of tiny notes playing and fading away endlessly.

How many sounds were there in the world? The flutter of wings as birds moved restlessly in sleep. The piping of insects, even through the pouring rain.

Sound came in waves, hundreds and thousands of waves, a tide breaking softly around Totoro, Satsuki, and Mei. Sound rose from the rain-soaked earth and poured from the branches shaken by the wind. Even the wordless, deepening darkness spoke to them.

*Here, here, here*

The heavens were an ocean of sound, rising and fading away, sounds without sound.

*Here*

*We are here*

*Here...*

"The bus!" Mei was wide awake. She tugged Satsuki's hand and pointed. A pair of headlights raced toward them. Satsuki gasped. The bus was moving so fast, it made a sound like the wind moaning.

Two bright headlights.

Not a bus. A cat.

It was a colossal cat, its eyes headlights. It hurtled toward them, dug its legs into the road, and came to a stop just beyond Totoro.

It dug its *twelve* legs into the road. It was a cat bus. It backed up like a giant centipede and turned its eyebeams toward Totoro. The roll sign read, "For Tsukamori."

Satsuki and Mei peered at the furry, striped bus in astonishment. Through the windows they could see passengers.

Little nature spirits. Sitting in the bus, here and there, just like people.

One of the windows widened into a door.

Totoro climbed in and the cat bus sped away, leaving Satsuki and Mei gaping with amazement. For a few moments they could see its yellow-green headlights flashing at odd angles, right, left, and toward the sky as it raced down the road and up and over the distant hills, until finally it was out of sight.

They were alone. Nothing moved in the night.

"Totoro took Daddy's umbrella," Satsuki said, still gaping.

Far down the road, another bus was coming toward them. A real bus.

It stopped in front of the girls with a squeal of brakes. The first person down the steps was Tatsuo.

Satsuki and Mei stared, not quite sure if he was real. His white cap glowed softly under streetlamp.

"Well! This is a surprise," Tatsuo said. Satsuki and Mei hugged his legs.

"We saw a cat bus, Daddy!" Mei shouted.

"It was scary!" Satsuki said.

"The cat bus—Daddy!—the cat bus took Totoro. Daddy! A great big cat, but it was a bus! Daddy! Daddy!" Mei couldn't contain her excitement.

Still holding his briefcase, Tatsuo squatted and

gave both girls a big hug. "I'm sorry I was late," he said. "You must have been really worried." He looked at them impishly.

"You know, I think I just squashed the croquettes in my briefcase. Shall we run home right now and find out?"

## 7. Totoro's Gift

When Satsuki woke the next morning she felt, more than remembered, the strange events of the previous day. Did it all really happen?

She tried to picture every detail.

The cat bus. It had come running up the road on twelve legs. The next thing they knew, Totoro was gone. Then the real bus had come. Tatsuo had gotten off. By then the rain had stopped. Everything seemed to go back to being commonplace and ordinary again.

As they were walking away, Satsuki had looked over her shoulder again and again, but the bus stop and the shrine no longer seemed special. The steel pole with its round sign looked forlorn in the yellow light from the streetlamp. Totoro had just been there, his gray fur glistening in the rain. Now the sign seemed to mock her. *That's right. Nothing special happened...*

Maybe it *was* a dream. Maybe she had just

nodded off for a second or two as she stood there with Mei on her back. That was all the time it would have taken to dream something.

Lying in the futon, Satsuki put her arms over her head and arched her back. It felt good to stretch.

She wondered what had happened to Tatsuo's umbrella. Sure enough, it was missing from its usual spot when they returned home. Totoro must've taken it after all. Where else could it have gone to?

Mei was still curled in a ball, breathing softly. Satsuki was careful not to wake her sister as she rose from her futon. She dressed quietly in the clothes she'd laid out next to her pillow the night before. She slid open the door and crept down the creaky-board hall, trying her best not to creak the boards.

In the kitchen, the charcoal stove was lit and the kettle was chuffing like a locomotive. The aroma of miso soup wafted from the pot. Tatsuo was chopping pickled cucumbers on the cutting board.

"Morning, Daddy."

"Good morning. You're up early," Tatsuo said. He glanced at his watch. "Breakfast will be ready in a bit."

Satsuki took her toothbrush from the cup by the sink and drew some water from the pump. "The weather looks nice today."

"Yep. No more rainy season," Tatsuo said.

"Can I help with anything?"

"Sure. Why don't you go get the paper?"

"You got it!" Satsuki said. She went to the front door and put her sandals on. Outside the sky was deep blue. The sun was still low in the sky but shining fiercely. The air was sweet and dry, but the grass was wet. There were little puddles here and there in the yard. Satsuki started thinking about Totoro again.

Where had the cat bus taken him? Was he back in Tsukamori Woods? She looked toward the giant laurel. Its branches were thick with foliage, like a cat with bristling fur. The leaves sparkled in the sun. The lower branches were thronged with birds and filled with a cacophony of twittering and chirping, like a joyous commentary on the weather.

Satsuki was just starting down the path to the road when she saw it.

Tatsuo's umbrella was halfway down the path. It was still open.

Her eyes widened in astonishment. For a moment, she wondered if she might not see Totoro step out from behind it.

Why was it here? Who had left it?

Heart pounding, she rushed down the path. She was going so fast, the umbrella moved a little as she ran up to it. A big, eight-lobed fatsia leaf lay on the ground, half-hidden by the umbrella. The leaf was strong and stiff, like Totoro's paws. Seeds from all kinds of trees were piled on the leaf: chinquapin and horse chestnut, oak and walnut, gingko, and of course zelkova.

"Look at all this!" Satsuki was delighted. She squatted down and let the seeds run through her fingers. *I wonder*, she thought. *I don't believe it. Can I believe it?*

The open umbrella. The leaf. The pile of seeds. Totoro hadn't known what an umbrella was. He wouldn't know how to close it.

*Did Totoro really do this? That would be so wonderful...*

Satsuki loved Totoro. He had been so kind to her and Mei. The umbrella had hardly been big enough to keep him dry, but he stood right next to her, holding it for the longest time, while she heard things she'd never heard before.

Satsuki picked up the umbrella and held it over her head like Totoro. The mysterious scent poured down on her. She knew it immediately. Dry grass. Mint. Lizard tail. Daisies. A little sharp and heavy. A little like sunshine. The scent of the woods. The scent of Totoro! She inhaled the fragrances eagerly and remembered.

"It *was* Totoro! He brought these seeds for us," Satsuki said aloud.

A drop of water fell from the branches and struck the umbrella with a dull plop. The sound was nothing like the wonderful music Satsuki had heard yesterday.

She folded the umbrella, put it under her arm, and picked up the fatsia leaf. Seeds spilled through the gaps between the lobes: slender oak acorns, round sawtooth acorns, shiny wild camellia seeds. Satsuki gathered them all up, put them safely in her pocket, and hurried back to the house.

"Mei! Mei!"

When Satsuki came pounding down the hall and threw open the storm shutters, Mei jumped up, startled. But when she saw the umbrella and the pile of seeds sitting on the step outside the veranda, she didn't seem at all surprised.

"Did Totoro come back?"

Satsuki goggled at her. "How did you know?"

"There was a big round jar in his house. It was full of seeds too," Mei said.

All that day at school, Satsuki's head was in the clouds. The only thing she could think about was Totoro. She doodled pictures of him in her notebook. She wrote a letter to her mother about him. She thought about writing a letter to Totoro himself. How would she address it? "To My Neighbor, Totoro." And what about the seeds? Were they supposed to do something with them?

"*Miss* Kusakabe. Would you be so kind as to tell me where your head has been all day?" Miss Moriyama's voice was calm, but it cut through the classroom buzz like a knife. Satsuki blushed and looked at her lap.

"Please explain, otherwise I'll thank you to change your attitude. Do you know why?" Miss Moriyama stared ominously around at the rest of the class.

"Because the scatterbrain bug is catching, especially for little brains that have trouble concentrating. I've seen it. It's horrible."

Satsuki couldn't just blab to anyone about Totoro. She sat up straight in her chair and tried to look properly attentive. But soon her head was back in the clouds. *What would it be like to ride the cat bus? Those claws sure were scary at first.* The more she basked in these thoughts, the more excited and feverish she became. This new world was so fascinating that she could hardly spare a thought for her lessons.

Perhaps unfortunately for Miss Moriyama, her fifth period lecture was "Cultivating Green Peas." Since most of the children were from farming families, and most of those families grew green peas, they didn't pay much attention. They didn't exactly mean to goof off, but everyone was talking to his or her seatmate. A few students even got up and walked around.

Satsuki didn't know the first thing about growing green peas, but... *Wait a minute!* Maybe she and Mei could take the seeds that Totoro had given them and plant them out in the garden? She and Mei could be tree farmers. She could picture it all very clearly.

As the lesson went on, the talking and noise-making gradually grew louder. Thanks to all the buzzing around her, Satsuki had no trouble imagining herself in the forest of trees she was going to grow. Gradually the classroom disappeared, and she was in a grove of stone oaks, camellias, and horse chestnuts. She was in a trance.

"Everyone on your feet!" Miss Moriyama sounded like a drill instructor.

"It's too late for spring fever. Summer vacation is weeks away. What's gotten into you? I have no idea, but I'm not going to waste your time or mine. You don't need my lessons. Go ahead, go out into the world with heads full of straw."

The children hung their heads in silence.

After that, Miss Moriyama had even more to say about green peas. It seemed like the day would never end.

When Satsuki finally got home, Mei, who had spent the day guarding the seeds, asked her to find a little pottery jar to keep them in, just the way Totoro did.

Satsuki had a different idea. She told Mei about the vision she had had during class. "Listen, Mei. Why don't we plant these seeds in the garden?"

Satsuki's plan went like this. She and Mei would clear a plot for the seeds. They would plant the seeds. The seeds would sprout. If they watered the seedlings, they would get bigger. All they would have to do was sit back and watch them grow.

Chinquapin seeds would grow chinquapin

trees. Oak seeds would become oaks. Chestnut seeds would turn into chestnuts, and someday the garden would be a forest.

"Trees don't grow fast. We'll get old," Mei said.

"That's all right," Satsuki said.

"What if we move away?"

"We can come back and visit the forest anytime."

"But what if it's too far?"

"What does it matter? Someone else can take care of it. Let's plant a garden, Mei. Let's grow a forest."

"I don't like gardens." Mei shook her head.

"Why? We can clear a spot next to the pine tree. There's nothing there now. It'll be fun."

"No it won't."

"But—why?"

Mei didn't have a good feeling about gardens. This was because of the vegetable garden Tatsuo had planted behind the house. It looked shabby and depressing.

The tomato and eggplant leaves were drooping. Insects had eaten them full of holes. Only three cucumber plants had come up. Tatsuo had put long stakes in the ground for the cucumber vines to climb, but they kept growing sideways instead of up, and there were so many stakes leaning at all angles that the garden looked like a porcupine. It was nothing like Granny's field, which was full of healthy-looking vegetables.

"I'm going to put these seeds away," said Mei.

"What's the point of that?" Satsuki was getting exasperated.

"Because I want to," Mei told her.

"But...uhm, see, we can plant the seeds and they'll grow into a forest—"

"I don't want a forest."

Satsuki played her last card. "Don't you want Totoro to come and live with us?" She looked sidelong at Mei.

"Totoro?" Mei pricked up her ears.

Now Satsuki had her. She went for the kill. "Of course. Why do you think he gave us all these seeds? We're supposed to make a forest. Then Totoro can live with us."

"In our garden?"

"Where else?"

Mei looked doubtful. "When's he coming?"

"Totoro? Oh, you know, when there's a big forest out there," Satsuki said vaguely.

"Will it grow soon?"

"Soon? Mmm...Sure, why not?" Satsuki smiled

weakly. She was starting to feel doubtful too, but for a different reason.

"Really?" Mei was overjoyed. "I'm going to make a garden. I decided." She looked expectantly at Satsuki, but there was no answer. "Come on, Satsuki. Let's start."

"Sure...we should do that." Satsuki was a little disgusted at herself for tricking her sister. "Listen, Mei. What'll you do if the seeds don't sprout right away?"

"It's okay. They grow fast."

"Seeds don't always sprout, you know."

"These ones will!"

So the two sisters made a little garden by the pine tree.

First they pulled all the weeds. Some of the weeds were taller than both of them. They cleared a space that was as close to a square as they could make it. That was enough work to make them sweaty and dirty.

Next they tilled the soil. Satsuki used a hoe. Mei used a little shovel. The soil was full of rocks. The sun was hot and the ground was muddy.

"Mei, I don't think this...this part of the garden," Satsuki said, panting, "used to be farmland." She was kicking rocks with her feet, the ones that were too big to pull out with her hands. She remembered what Granny Ogaki had told Tatsuo when he planted his vegetables behind the house. "This used to be farmland. Good soil for growing things."

The soil near the pine tree was hard. It was difficult for a child to dig more than a few inches into it. The space they cleared wasn't much bigger than a flower bed. As the sun sank low and the late afternoon breeze began to blow, Satsuki gathered all the rocks and used them to make a border around the plot.

Finally they dug little holes with their fingers, filled them with water from the watering can, and dropped a seed in each one. They covered the seeds with loose earth.

"Mei, don't plant them so close together," Satsuki said.

The well-watered plot looked impressive and beautiful after they planted all of Totoro's seeds in three slightly crooked rows. The black earth seemed to promise that the seeds would sprout and grow into a giant forest.

"After they start growing, we can replant some of them farther away to make more room," Satsuki said. She believed in Totoro. His seeds were certain to grow.

Every day they watered the seeds and waited for them to come up out of the soil. Whenever Mei went into the garden to play, she would pay a visit to the little plot and squat next to the rock border, searching for signs of life. After a few days, Satsuki began to worry that Mei would call her a liar and demand to know why nothing was growing.

When Granny saw what they had done, she told them, "It's the wrong time of year for planting trees. You come by the house. You can take some rose balsam and plant it right here. The purple flowers are pretty."

Still, the children were determined to have a forest, and they watered the seeds every day. But as the days passed and June became July with no signs of life, they began to give up hope. Perhaps the seeds wanted to stay hidden forever.

Still, they were Totoro's gift. They must be different from ordinary seeds. No matter how long it took, Satsuki and Mei would keep watching and watering them.

The night of the full moon came. The frogs in the grass sang a midsummer chorus. Crickets chirped from shadows beneath the bushes. A lone cicada, reluctant to go to sleep, trilled from its perch halfway up a tree. The night was hot and humid. It was well past midnight.

The moon shone down on the haunted house of Matsugo with a soft, mysterious glow. Its light came from the garden through the open storm shutter, flowed through the mosquito netting Tatsuo had set up for the first time this year, and caressed the sleeping forms of Satsuki and Mei.

A cool breeze whispered through the open shutter. The green netting swayed gently. The little bell Satsuki had hung under the eaves tinkled softly.

Satsuki wasn't sure whether it was the moonlight or the bell that woke her suddenly. When she opened her eyes, she was enveloped in sound that seemed to fill the night sky.

At first she thought she might be dreaming. Perhaps there was a festival going on in the village? She could hear the comical, rustic tones of a flute. Its music seemed to float somewhere above the roof. There was a deep, regular reverberation, like someone pounding on a huge drum, or a metronome for a symphony played by the leaves of the forest, the croaking of the frogs, and the gurgling of the stream.

Curious and still half asleep, Satsuki turned over

My Neighbor Totoro

on her stomach and peered out into the garden.

Totoro was there, in the garden, in the moonlight! Not just Totoro, but *totoros*—two little creatures who looked very much like him. They were marching around the seedbed!

She reached over and shook Mei awake. "Wake up, Mei. It's Totoro. He's in the garden!"

To Satsuki, it looked like the whole garden was swaying and moving in a mysterious night festival. The full moon peeked over the Tsukamori laurel, peering down at Totoro and his companions as they formed a strange procession.

"He's got the umbrella." Satsuki's voice was hoarse with surprise. How did he get hold of Tatsuo's umbrella again?

"They like umbrellas," Mei said. The girls squinted. The smallest totoro held the stem of a sprout in its mouth, with the leaf over its milky white body like an umbrella. Its larger companion was blue and held a lotus leaf over his head. There wasn't a hint of rain, but that didn't seem to matter a bit. Umbrellas seemed to have caught on with the totoros.

The creatures marched solemnly around the seedbed, large, medium, and small. Sometimes they leaped soundlessly from one end to the other. Where they landed, soot sprites, like pitch-black dandelion fluff, would scatter and rise into the sky.

Like something in a dream, the creatures leaped lightly over the seeds again and again. Each time they came to rest, the red zinnias near the pine tree would open and close, open and close.

Satsuki and Mei leaped from their beds and dashed outside into the cool silky breeze. They stretched their arms toward the starry sky and ran barefoot across the grass to Totoro.

*Come, now come, frolic and dance*
*On a night like this*
*No one can keep still*

The wind swirled around them. The branches of the trees bent up and down, hurrying the soot sprites on their way into the sky. Mint and lizard tail. Dry grass and daisies. The smell of sunshine under a full moon.

The totoros stood in a row by the seedbed. They were looking intently at something.

Satsuki and Mei saw transparent, delicate foam rising into the air out of the ground. Astonished, the girls watched as Totoro and his little companions begin to play with the foam.

Right away, Mei imitated them. She began batting the foam around with both hands.

Totoro used his long claws to spin the translucent, ice-colored foam into long white chains. Fascinated, Satsuki imitated Totoro as he drew the foam into long strands and threw them all over the garden. The foam was pleasantly cool to the touch, and to Satsuki, it was heavier than it looked. Soon the garden was decked with beautiful, lacy strands of foam that glowed golden in the moonlight and swayed in the breeze.

"Look, Mei," Satsuki said. "All the trees in the garden look like Christmas trees!"

Totoro gave a strange call, like tree trunks creaking in the wind. The foam disappeared and the garden grew silent.

Totoro's ears twitched as if they had caught something faint. Satsuki knew immediately—though she did not know why—that Totoro had heard a voice in the earth and was answering.

It was the seeds. Tiny sprouts were emerging from the ground, as if from Granny Ogaki's best black earth. They heard Totoro's voice. *Come out*, he told them. *The moon is full. The wind is moving. The warm, beautiful summer is waiting for you.*

Satsuki and Mei sat on the ground next to the seedbed in their pajamas. They stroked the earth and spoke to it the way Totoro did. They spoke to the gingko and the zelkova seeds, and the seed of the chinquapin, which would one day grow into a giant tree. *Come out. Come out. We'll take good care of you, so please come out.* They were filled with a joy that surpassed that of any game they had ever played.

The seeds heard the voices of Satsuki and Mei. The earth writhed in answer beneath their palms.

"Here they come!" Satsuki shouted.

The girls giggled joyfully as tiny hands reached up from below to touch theirs. The beautiful little sprouts peeked from the soil, then shot upward as if eager to be with Satsuki and Mei. Before their eyes, the sprouts grew into seedlings with delicate, yellow-green leaves, then into young trees. They kept growing, soaring toward the sky, leaves rustling in the wind.

Totoro leaped once more and landed soundlessly, followed by the two little totoros. Suddenly the moon rose up from behind the laurel as if to say, our festival is over. Slowly, very slowly, it moved westward across the sky.

*Come, now come, frolic and dance*
*On a night like this*
*No one can keep still*

The moon and the trees, the grass and the flowers sang amid the soft, cool breeze. But Satsuki and Mei weren't listening. They watched in a daze as the totoros flew away into the starry sky.

The girls woke at the same time that morning. In an instant they were running to check the seeds.

"What do you think we'll find, Mei?" Satsuki called to her. "Sprouts or no sprouts?"

"Sprouts!" Mei shouted. "Totoro was here!"

They knelt on the ground and peered at the seedbed. There they were!

A tiny forest reached for the morning sun—the shining faces of the trees to come, in three crooked rows sprouting from the earth.

## 8. Summer Vacation

"Oh no!"

Kanta Ogaki squinted anxiously down the road from his vantage point in the garden, half hidden behind the compost pile. Tatsuo Kusakabe was coming toward him, flanked by his daughters. The girls were dressed for some kind of outing. It wasn't even seven in the morning yet.

Satsuki looked happy walking next to her father. Her short hair was fluffed out. She was wearing a white outfit with a sailor collar trimmed in blue, a narrow-brimmed white hat and sandals. She was carrying a large wicker suitcase. Mei was wearing a yellow hat, a red- and green-checked dress, and red leather shoes with white socks. She was carrying a green cloth backpack. The backpack looked stuffed.

*Just like a couple of city kids*, Kanta thought as he watched them from behind the compost, mouth agape. He scurried into the house.

*Not now.* He was panicking. *Of all the times to come!*

It was Kanta's job to muck the stable in the morning. He had just been hauling yesterday's soiled straw to the compost pile in a wheelbarrow. It was smelly work, especially in summer. Very smelly. And now Mr. Archaeologist and his daughters from the haunted house decided to turn up, wearing their Sunday best.

Kanta was so distracted that he almost knocked down his grandmother on the way to his room. He skidded to a stop in astonishment. Granny was dressed in a summer kimono and was putting on her sash.

"What's going on, Granny? Are you going out?"

Granny Ogaki wrapped the brown sash tight around her waist. Kanta almost never saw her dressed like this. She looked completely different.

"I'm off to Shichikokuyama Hospital," Granny said.

"Why? Are you sick?"

"Of course not. Satsuki and Mei are spending ten days with their mother's relatives in Tokyo. They can't very well leave without paying their respects, now can they? I'm going along with them."

Kanta snorted. "How come their dad doesn't take 'em himself?"

"He's very busy, Kanta. He has to be away from the house for a few days."

Granny was just asking Kanta whether he wanted to go along when the sliding front door rattled open and a voice came from the entryway.

"Good morning. We're here."

Kanta peeked out and saw Satsuki, Tatsuo, and Mei standing on the threshold. He ducked back inside, frozen with panic. Granny tucked her coin purse into her sash and took a cloth-wrapped parcel from the sideboard. "Coming! Good morning," she called.

Kanta heard Tatsuo say, "We're so sorry to trouble you again. We really appreciate your help." He was being very polite, but he sounded as if he was in a hurry.

"Oh, don't give it a second thought. I'm happy to be of help. It's not far. I've been wanting to meet your wife and give her my regards," Granny said.

Kanta looked at the garden as he eavesdropped. It was going to be a beautiful day. He wondered what Satsuki's mother was like. Maybe it would be fun to meet her.

He scowled. His mother had recently bought

him a pair of trousers for special occasions, but the legs were so baggy they almost looked like a skirt. He decided he'd rather shovel manure than dress up like that.

"Now, I hope you two don't mind taking the train by yourselves," Tatsuo was saying to Satsuki.

"Don't worry. We'll be fine," she answered, but Kanta thought she sounded anything but confident.

"Give me a call in ten days and let me know what time you want me to come get you," Tatsuo said. "Aunt Kyoko has the number where I'll be staying. If you need to talk to me, just ask her. Mei! What are you doing? Come back here."

Mei had taken an interest in Kanta's wheelbarrow just outside the door. She had grabbed the handles and was toddling off toward the compost pile, pushing it in front of her.

"Mei! I'm leaving. Come say goodbye." He turned to Satsuki. "Your grandmother will be waiting for you on the platform when you get there. Be sure to get in the third car from the front, so she can find you right away. I guess I told you that already, didn't I."

"Daddy, call us once while you're away, okay?" Satsuki said. "Even twice."

"Will do. Granny, I'll leave them in your good hands, then. I better be off." He said goodbye to Satsuki and Mei and walked quickly down the path.

"Well now," Granny said, "we'd better be going ourselves. The bus will be along soon."

Kanta felt oddly disappointed after they left. He went into the living room and flopped listlessly on the tatami. His mother and brothers would be back from weeding the field soon. He was starving. Why didn't they hurry up?

Life was no fun.

When Granny saw Satsuki and Mei draped over their mother at the hospital, she smiled and said quietly, "Why, the two of you are just like babes in your mother's arms."

Visitors were usually not allowed in the morning. Yasuko spoke quietly too. "Thank you for bringing them. I hope it wasn't too much trouble."

"Oh, that's all right. Satsuki and Mei are such good little girls, it's no trouble at all."

Yasuko quickly combed Satsuki's hair. She took two ribbons from the drawer next to her bed and decorated Mei's ponytails.

"Tell your grandmother not to worry. I'll be out of the hospital soon," Yasuko said. She seemed a bit nervous about the visit her daughters were about to make.

"Pick a place to put your train ticket and keep it there.

"Mei, listen to what your sister tells you.

"Satsuki, I want you and Mei to be big girls and not expect too much help from Yoné and Fumi. They're very busy.

"And remember, don't talk back."

Yasuko saw them to the door of the hospital. "Take good care of yourselves, both of you. Be careful not to take the wrong train."

It brought tears of pity to Granny's eyes to see how Yasuko stroked Mei's cheek and hugged Satsuki as they said goodbye. It must break their mother's heart to have to be apart from these adorable little girls for so long.

"Don't worry about a thing, Mrs. Kusakabe. I'll see they get on the train. Their grandmother will be waiting when they get there. Everything will be fine."

As they left the hospital, Satsuki was glad they had gone to see their mother. Yasuko had told them she would probably be allowed to come home for one or two days during the summer vacation. Tatsuo would be home from his fieldwork on the day Satsuki and Mei came back from Tokyo. Satsuki was a little nervous about the prospect of ten days with the Terashimas without their mother. But at least when she and Mei came back, the family would be together. The thought made her resolve to make the best of the ten days in Tokyo.

"Put this in your backpack, Mei. It's from your mother," Granny said and gave her a small box wrapped in paper.

"Is it something to eat?"

"Rice cakes. You can eat them in the train if you're careful not to make a mess."

When they arrived at the station, Granny bought their tickets. When Satsuki tried to pay, Granny shook her head and smiled. "Don't worry about it, dear. When you get to Tokyo, buy yourself a nice magazine to read."

The train soon pulled in to the station. It was empty. Just as planned, they went to the third car from the front. Satsuki waited by the door, but it didn't open. Granny opened it for her. Satsuki was surprised.

"Granny, isn't it supposed to open by itself?

What happens if we get to Tokyo and I can't get it open in time and the train leaves again?"

"Don't you worry. Once you get to the next station, the doors will open on their own."

They had never taken such a long ride on the train by themselves before, and Satsuki was feeling very tense.

The departure bell started ringing. Satsuki and Mei got on the train. "Thank you, Granny," Satsuki said. Granny said goodbye and closed the door. The train jolted forward. Granny smiled and waved. Soon she was out of sight. The girls sat down and looked silently out the window.

It was an hour and fifteen minutes to their destination. They began to relax a little as the train rolled along. They munched on rice cakes and timidly visited the next car, looking for a bin to throw away the wrappings.

Gradually the forest scenery disappeared, followed by the farmland as they got closer to Tokyo. Gray-tiled houses stood clustered together. Soon there was nothing but houses and buildings crowding the tracks on both sides. The dirty neon signs, switched off for the day, made Satsuki feel nostalgic.

When the train arrived at their station and they stepped onto the platform, Yasuko's mother was waiting for them with Yuriko, their cousin. Yuriko was Satsuki's age.

"Gramma!" Mei was overjoyed. She'd never left Satsuki's side on the train, but now she let go of her sister's hand and ran across the platform to Mrs. Terashima, her little legs pumping so hard that she nearly fell down. She threw her arms around her grandmother.

Yasuko and Mei had parted when Mei was only three years old. Ever since, Mrs. Terashima had lavished affection on the lonely little girl. Mei loved her grandmother fiercely and basked in her affection. She was even more herself with Gramma than with Satsuki.

Mrs. Terashima bundled everyone into a taxi and took them to a department store in Ginza. The ninth floor was full of restaurants. The largest one had a display case with wax models of the dishes on the menu. As they stood outside the restaurant, Mrs. Terashima said, "Let's have a nice lunch. What would you like?"

Mei's eyes widened when she saw the display case. She pressed her nose against the glass.

"I want...I want...ice cream!"

"That's dessert," Mrs. Terashima said. "What would you like for lunch, Mei?"

"I want...uhm, that one, with the flag."

"The child plate. That's a good choice. What would you like, Satsuki?"

Satsuki didn't feel comfortable choosing a dish if her grandmother was going to treat. She finally said, "I'll have what Mei's having."

"The child plate? Are you sure that's what you'd like?"

"Mm-hmm."

Yuriko tugged excitedly at her grandmother's sleeve. "Can I have the broiled eel?"

"Certainly, Yuriko. Calm down. Satsuki, you don't dislike eel, do you?"

"No," Satsuki said.

"Then the three of us can have the eel, and Mei can have the child's plate. How does that sound?"

After lunch Mrs. Terashima took them to the eighth floor. The whole floor was devoted to toys. There were gaily flashing lights and windup toys playing musical instruments. Mei was almost beside herself with excitement. She pointed to the first doll she saw, cried "I want it!" and tugged at her grandmother's hand. She saw a toy train. "Please buy it!"

"Don't be so selfish, Mei," Satsuki scolded her. "It's not polite."

Mei puffed out her cheeks in frustration. "But I want it."

"It's all right, Satsuki," Mrs. Terashima said. "Today is a special day. I haven't seen either of you for so long. If you'd like something, just tell me. It's my pleasure."

Satsuki nodded and said, "Thank you, Grandmother." She and her cousin walked over to a display of dolls. Satsuki had grown up with Yuriko and they were close friends.

"Satsuki," said Yuriko, "do they have Bottle Baby where you live?"

Bottle Baby was a big fad. It was made from soft rubber and looked a bit like a Kewpie doll. It wore a diaper and could "drink" from a little bottle filled with water.

"Nope," Satsuki said as she gazed longingly at the dolls. "There's only one store in Matsugo. You can get pens and pencils, and miso, and canned food. They sell vegetables too. All kinds of everyday stuff. But they don't have much for kids. Maybe just fireworks."

Yuriko looked astonished. "You really do live in the sticks."

"Yeah."

"Isn't it boring?"

Satsuki had never thought about it. "No, it's not boring. Not really."

Mrs. Terashima urged Satsuki to choose something, but in the end Satsuki couldn't bring herself to do it. She wasn't trying to be obstinate, but she felt sorry for Yuriko. It didn't feel right unless they both got something. If she'd been little, like Mei, that would have been different. But Satsuki was in the fourth grade, and the thought of acting selfish embarrassed her.

"What about me?" Yuriko ventured several times, but Mrs. Terashima would just say, "Don't you already have all the toys you need?"

After the toy store, they went shopping for clothes. Mrs. Terashima showered them with new clothes. Pants and shirts and chemises. Socks and blouses and skirts. She bought them several pretty dresses. Everything was smart and chic.

When Satsuki said that they had brought plenty of clothing, Mrs. Terashima told her, "Nonsense. I peeked in Mei's backpack. Everything looked rather wilted to me. Yasuko hasn't been able to look after you the way she would if she were healthy. It's not her fault, but I must say, I was shocked."

There were so many purchases to take home

that Mrs. Terashima had to hire an extra-large taxi. She looked a little tired. "This is a special day," she said.

When they arrived at the Terashima house, Satsuki and Mei ran excitedly into the entryway, shouting and laughing. It had been so long!

"I'm home!" they each called, as if they still lived there. They threw off their shoes, stepped up into the house, and slipped and slid down the polished wood of the hall to the foot of the stairs. Aunt Kyoko was just coming down.

"No children on the second floor," she said. "You'll be staying with Mother in the cottage." She went to the entryway and looked out. Mrs. Terashima was just paying for the taxi.

"What a lot of packages. Fumi!" Aunt Kyoko called. "Come out here, please. Mother's back. She needs some help."

Satsuki and Mei slipped into the wooden garden sandals, which were much too big for them, and went through the garden to Mrs. Terashima's cottage. The room where they used to live on the second floor had been taken over by Uncle Terashima and Aunt Kyoko. This wasn't Satsuki and Mei's house anymore. Of course that couldn't be helped.

Still, every day was like a birthday. Satsuki explored the books in the bookstore. Mei's grandmother took her to the neighborhood sweet shop. One day Aunt Kyoko took them to see a movie, and once Uncle took them to the amusement park.

Today was another special day. Dinner was sukiyaki, to be cooked at the dining table on a portable gas burner. Everyone was excited. Yoné and Fumi hurried back and forth down the long corridor between the living room and the kitchen, carrying big plates heaped with the makings for sukiyaki—thin-sliced beef, mushrooms, vegetables, and tofu.

"Be patient, Miss Satsuki. Dinner will be here soon," good-natured Fumi said as she hurried back to the kitchen for more. How could there be more? Satsuki wondered. Maybe Fumi was going to bring the rice.

Satsuki sat on the tatami, waiting for the rest of the household. She wished she could help in the kitchen, but the one time she had offered, Yoné told her, "You'd just be in the way." Yoné and Fumi handled all the housework. There was nothing for anyone else to do.

Satsuki had even finished her summer homework.

To pass the time she took a match from the box on the table, turned the valve on the gas burner, and lit the flame. The gas caught with a whoosh, and a circle of pretty blue-white flame appeared.

*This is so easy,* she thought. *Just strike the match.* She was thinking about the kitchen in the haunted house. With this gas burner, you could have any size flame you wanted. And no smoke.

"Satsuki, what on earth are you doing?" Aunt Kyoko snatched the box of matches out of her hand. Startled, Satsuki jumped to her feet. Her aunt looked furious.

"You know better than to play with fire. You might influence the other children. You're in the fourth grade now. You're too old for such foolishness."

Play with fire?

Satsuki didn't know how to answer. All she could do was look away, embarrassed. Unfortunately, this only made Aunt Kyoko angrier.

Satsuki used matches morning and night in Matsugo. She worked hard to get the fire for the bath and for cooking just right. Cooking with fire was far harder than cooking with gas, but she knew how to use it to make miso soup, rice, and grilled fish. And every day she built a fire for the bath, coaxing the flames until the wood crackled and filled the room with its sweet aroma. But there was no way her aunt would listen to anything she had to say.

Aunt Kyoko lowered her voice.

"Satsuki, I'm concerned. What's happened to you and Mei since you moved to Matsugo? I'm very disappointed in you. You walk around in the house without your slippers. Your speech is careless. I think your mother would be heartbroken if she could see how you're behaving.

"Mei's just as bad. Uncle was devastated when he saw what she did to his bonsai. She climbs trees. She walks into the pond and chases the fish. She crawled under the hedge into the next yard. Yuriko would never do anything like that. What makes you different? I don't know what's wrong, but please don't play with fire again in this house." She stalked out of the room.

*Don't talk back.*

That's what Yasuko had said the day they left for Tokyo. *Well,* Satsuki thought, *I couldn't talk back if I tried.* How could she begin to explain her point of view? Or Mei's?

In Matsugo, the kids crawled under and over

whatever they liked, and no one said anything. Satsuki knew she could never make Aunt Kyoko understand that. She'd just say, "What's wrong is wrong. Just because you don't get in trouble doesn't make it all right." What could Satsuki say? No matter what, Aunt Kyoko always won.

Satsuki was starting to wish she could go home.

She wondered how Totoro's trees were doing. Maybe she'd come home to find a forest in the backyard.

Her thoughts wandered from Totoro's trees to Uncle's prize bonsai. The memory made her wince. Mei had yanked the little pine tree out of its pot and clumsily tried to replant it in the backyard. When Aunt and Uncle confronted her, she told them angrily that trees were supposed to grow in the ground, not in little pots. When they didn't understand, she threw herself on the floor and cried her eyes out. It had been terribly embarrassing. Mrs. Terashima had tried her best to calm Mei down, but this time at least, Mei didn't deserve anyone's sympathy.

Still, Satsuki had to admit that every day of their visit had been fun. Life was convenient, clean, and easy. Easy was good. It was very good.

Beautiful starched sheets. Light summer comforters with sparkling white covers. Rice with every meal, without lifting a finger.

Life in Matsugo was very inconvenient.

*I wonder what Kanta's up to?*

For some reason, she suddenly thought of Kanta. She wondered what he would say if she told him what Aunt Kyoko said about playing with fire. He'd probably just roll his eyes as if he had no idea what she was talking about. No idea.

The haunted house had been empty for a week. Kanta was feeling a bit lonely. So far he had spent most of his vacation loafing and avoiding his chores. Every day from morning to dusk, he roamed all over Matsugo with his friends. Kanta's vacations were packed with activity. He begrudged the sun going down. If it were daylight all the time, he thought grumpily, he would have that many more hours in the day to play.

Today he'd been for a swim in the river. Tomorrow he was going to the hills behind his house to set bird traps. Next day he'd be up on Mount Haké. The day after that was Tsukamori Woods, and after that, fishing in the pond. He was a busy guy. He didn't have time to warm a chair or waste time on summer assignments. But now and then things would get a little slow.

It was two o'clock. The sun beat down. Everything was quiet. The village and its people, the cows and the horses were taking refuge from the heat. Kanta was sprawled on the floor reading a comic book when his six-year-old brother Shigeta wandered in. Shigeta had just completed his first half-year of elementary school.

"Is Satsuki back?" he said to his brother.

Kanta was startled. "What makes you think she's back?"

"I heard people talking."

"Go out to the road and see if you can see anything," Kanta said.

An order was an order. Shigeta ran outside and came back. "I didn't see anybody," he said. But Kanta's curiosity was aroused. He had to be sure.

"Shigeta, go over to Satsuki's and see if she's back."

"No way!" This was reasonable. Shigeta had to stand up for himself occasionally.

"You said she was back. She better be back," Kanta grumbled and got up off the floor. He went to the entryway and picked up his cicada pole.

Shigeta watched him anxiously. "Where are you going?"

"Tsukamori," Kanta said casually.

"For cicadas?"

"Yep."

"Wait, I'm coming too."

As they walked up the road toward the woods, Shigeta said, "So, what about Satsuki's house?"

"After we catch some cicadas," Kanta said.

Soon they could see the Tsukamori laurel. "Let's walk in the creek," Kanta said. "It's nice and cool." Walking in the creek would also wash off some dirt and dust and make them more presentable. Kanta remembered how Satsuki had been dressed when she left for Tokyo. He was beginning to think it might pay to take better care of his appearance.

It felt good walking in the creek. Kanta was in a good mood. Nonchalantly, he scanned the haunted house for signs of life.

Until Satsuki arrived, the house had been Kanta's stomping grounds. Because his grandmother was looking after the property, it was natural for him to be there, and in any case an empty house and yard are always a magnet for children. Kanta and his friends played Tarzan and pretended the cranberry thicket with its tunnels was a secret base. He and his friends were in and out of the yard all the time.

Once the high-class Kusakabe family moved in, the haunted house became something of a mystery for Kanta and the other children. Maybe this would be a good time to see if anything had changed.

"Let's check it out!" Kanta said. With Shigeta bringing up the rear, Kanta crossed the footbridge and walked up the path to the yard. The cicadas in the branches above the path were shrieking so loud it almost hurt.

As soon as he reached the top of the path, Kanta knew the house was still empty. The grass had grown taller and thicker since he'd trimmed it for Granny. The vines and creepers had spread rapidly. No one seemed to be caring for the garden. Insects called raucously from the grass. The shut-tered house and its yard really did look haunted.

Satsuki's wavy hair looked nice when the wind blew it, Kanta thought. The house with its Western-style design was the perfect backdrop for Satsuki with her smart clothes, and her little sister with the foreign-sounding name. That is, if only they were here.

"Hey, Kanta, look at this!" Shigeta waved to him from over by the pine tree. "I found something funny!"

Kanta ran to see what his brother was looking at. It was a little sign on a stick, stuck in the ground next to a plot like a flower bed, with rocks around the edge.

Kanta read the sign out loud. "'This will be a forest someday. Please wait.' What's that supposed to mean?"

The plot was full of weeds. Kanta pushed them aside, wondering if anything else was growing there. Down among the weeds he found little seedlings coming up from the soil. *These are trees,* he thought. He scratched his head and read the sign again.

THIS WILL BE A FOREST SOMEDAY.
PLEASE WAIT.

Satsuki's handwriting was nice. He could almost hear her voice.

"They're doing this wrong," he said. He pushed the weeds aside and found more seedlings—oak and yew, black pine and cedar, zelkova and walnut. "Where did they get the seeds from?" He shook his head and began skillfully clearing the weeds from around the little trees. "Shigeta, go find a bucket and bring me some water."

*They need better drainage. Let's dig a trough around them,* Kanta thought. *If I do that much, Satsuki and Mei just have to come back.*

## 9. Mei Goes Missing

The song of the cicadas split the sky above the Tsukamori laurel.

"Can you believe how hot it is?" Miyoko was watching the shadow of a dragonfly hovering over the bleached ground.

"Yup," Kazuko said. She dipped her bare foot in the water-filled trough and watched it dry in the sun, over and over.

Kazuko and Miyoko were sitting by the pump in the backyard of the haunted mansion. They were cooling a big watermelon, and their feet, in the water trough. For more than two hours, they had been waiting for Satsuki to come back from Tokyo.

Miyoko put her hand on the watermelon. "It's getting nice and cold."

Of course the girls hadn't just been sitting here since noon. They had walked to the Fox Grove bus stop three times to see if Satsuki would be on the next bus. When she didn't show, they walked back to the haunted house and pumped more cold water into the trough. Since they didn't know when Satsuki was going to be back, they weren't sure how many times they'd have to wait at the bus stop.

"Shall we go again?" Miyoko said.

"Sure! Let's go." Kazuko kicked her wet feet into her sneakers.

After Miyoko pumped more cold water into the trough, they set off. The dragonfly resting in the nearby grass hummed into the air.

At Fox Grove, the bus pulled up to the stop.

"Oh, it smells like Matsugo!" Satsuki cried happily as she stepped down from the bus. "Hey, what are you guys doing here?" she said when she saw Miyoko and Kazuko standing under the trees.

Satsuki was wearing a frilly yellow dress and a bolero hat that Mrs. Terashima had selected. She looked like a French doll. Her wavy hair was held in place with a narrow ribbon the same color as the dress.

"Yup, Granny Ogaki, she told us you were, uhm, coming back today. Didn't she, Kazuko?" Miyoko said.

After waiting all this time, the girls felt suddenly embarrassed. "So my mother told us we should wait for you, and, uhm, she got a watermelon, and we took it over to Granny Ogaki's—no, I mean, your house, yup," Miyoko stammered.

Miyoko's bobbed, jet-black hair was dusty from walking back and forth between the bus stop and Satsuki's house. Gentle Kazuko just smiled. She was dripping with perspiration.

"Well, hello there. Is this the welcoming party?" Tatsuo said as he climbed down the steps. Satsuki smiled happily. Two of her friends had come to meet her! Tatsuo set down the heavy trunk and briefcase he was carrying. "Thanks for coming on such a hot day. How did you know which bus we were on? Hope you haven't been waiting here long."

"We came a few times. Didn't we?" Miyoko looked at Kazuko.

"Yup, this is the fourth time." Kazuko nodded.

Miyoko smiled. She didn't usually speak to Tatsuo. His white cap, wire-rimmed glasses, and pale skin made him seem stylish. He was different from the teachers at school. Miyoko was always a little tense around him.

As they walked along, Miyoko told Satsuki, "There's a watermelon back at your house. We're getting it cold." Satsuki was pleased. She turned and looked back at Tatsuo. "Daddy, Miyoko and Kazuko brought a watermelon for us."

Miyoko wondered how Satsuki could speak so casually to her father. Of course, he was her father. But things were different at Miyoko's house.

Everyone walked slowly so Mei didn't have to run. Tatsuo looked down at her. "Mei, there's cold watermelon waiting for us when we get back. What do you think of that?"

*Nothing has changed in my old home town*
*Flowers blooming, birds singing, the cool*
*    breeze*

The children spread out over the road, sometimes walking ahead of Tatsuo, sometimes trailing behind. They walked out of the coolness of the zelkova grove into the flat white heat of the village road.

"Hey you guys, I've got something for you too," Satsuki said.

Mei was holding Kazuko's hand. "Chocolate!" she yelled. "Bronson chocolate! And, and…fruit candy from Eikokuya Fruit Parlor! Gramma gave us lots of stuff for presents."

Kazuko looked a little puzzled. She wasn't sure if she knew what kind of presents these were.

They stopped along the way to thank Granny for her help. Tatsuo gave her a box of fine green tea, a present from his mother-in-law. Then they walked on toward the haunted house.

It was the hottest hour of the day, and the road was nearly deserted. The few people they did meet all said, "Welcome back." Everyone knew today was the day that the professor and his daughters would return from Tokyo. Word traveled fast in the small village.

When they got to the house, Tatsuo hurried to throw open the shutters and windows. "It sure is good to be home," he said.

Satsuki and Mei agreed completely. The house was shabby and the tatami mats were worn, but with the storm shutters thrown back, the rooms were just as bright and sunny as the overgrown garden. A cool breeze blew through the house. The startled dragonfly darted in and out of the study.

Satsuki was glad to be back. She put her bags in Mommy's room and hurried out to the garden. She was worried about Totoro's seedlings.

The plot was probably full of weeds by now,

like the rest of the yard. *Maybe I won't be able to tell the trees from the weeds*, she thought.

But when she got there, the plot looked completely different from the rest of the yard. Everything was tidier and more orderly than when they had left. In fact, it was a complete makeover.

Someone had dug a trench about eight inches wide around the edge of the plot. There was still a little water in the bottom. The plot looked moist and well-watered. The rest of the yard was parched, but here the soil was black and glistening.

Satsuki's sign was attached to a new length of green bamboo. Someone had cut angled slots in the bamboo to hold the top and bottom edges of the sign. The seedlings looked happy in the bright sunlight. All the weeds were gone. The plot was immaculate.

"Satsuki, let's open presents!" Mei called from the house.

"Okay," Satsuki called over her shoulder. She took one more look at the seedlings and ran to the pump. "C'mon, guys, let's eat," she said to Kazuko and Miyoko.

"Should we bring the watermelon?" Miyoko said. Kazuko was busy pumping cold water over it.

"That's the biggest watermelon I've ever seen,"

said Satsuki. She tried to pick it up, but it slipped and slid away from her in the water.

"You should change your clothes," said Kazuko. "You'll get your nice dress wet. We brought a net. We'll bring it into the kitchen for you."

"Okay. I'll ask my dad to cut it for us."

Satsuki ran back to the house. Miyoko and Kazuko exchanged glances, happy and a little scared. Another chance to talk to the professor.

They ate the watermelon in the breezy living room.

"Here's the chocolate." Satsuki gave each of her friends a slab of imported chocolate. The wrapper had a photo of a little blonde girl.

"How many?" Tatsuo had assigned Mei to divide up the fruit candy. "Is it right?" She had five pieces of candy in each little hand.

"That's right, five," Satsuki said.

"And there's three more each for us to eat right now," Tatsuo said. "So how many is that all together?" he asked Mei.

"Eight!" Miyoko blurted out. The candy was wrapped in pretty paper: gold, pink, blue-green, a rainbow of colors. Each girl had her own opinion about how the candy should be divided up. One wanted at least two gold and two green, another wanted one of each color. It was hard to decide.

"Better eat the watermelon before it gets warm," Tatsuo said.

The children each took a slice of watermelon, but their eyes were still on the chocolate and fruit candy.

"Is this watermelon from your garden?" Tatsuo asked Miyoko. She nodded and looked at Satsuki.

"Satsuki, can I take the other three candies home with me?"

Kazuko had just popped a candy in her mouth. She hurriedly took it out, looked at it sadly, and put it back.

As Satsuki munched on her watermelon she said, "Do you know who took care of our garden, out by the pine tree? Was that you?"

"No." Miyoko shook her head emphatically. "That was Kanta. Kanta was here every day."


The little seedlings cast shadows in the moonlight and trembled in the warm, gentle breeze. Satsuki stroked them with a fingertip.

"Grow big and strong," she whispered. She hadn't had time to greet her seedlings properly until now. "It must feel good to have everything so nice and neat. I better remember to thank Kanta for this."

Tatsuo was in the study organizing his field notes. Mei was busy too, carefully arranging her loot in her toy box—a deck of cards, a Chinese checkers set, and other treasures. Mommy would soon be back, and her room had to be neat.

Satsuki felt a deep sense of peace as she stroked the seedlings. She wished they would grow into a forest soon. "Grow big and strong. We're waiting for you."

In fact, the seedlings didn't seem to have gotten any bigger since the sisters had left for Tokyo. "I guess Totoro didn't come while we were gone," Satsuki said. "Otherwise I'm sure you'd all be three times bigger."

The night was lovely. The seedlings huddled close to the ground. They looked almost apologetic for not being bigger already.

Next day, Satsuki drew up a cleaning plan and posted it on the wall in the living room. She wanted the house to be spotless when Yasuko came home from the hospital. After their ten days with the Terashimas, the haunted house looked dirty, inconvenient, and uncomfortable. Mommy's visit was special, and Satsuki wanted her to have fun.

She had to get her summer assignment in shape to turn in too. It was time to buckle down and get to work.

August twentieth. Yasuko would be home in six days. First on the list: clean the kitchen. Miyoko and Kazuo dropped by to help. The three girls wiped everything down, though when Satsuki tried to wipe down the stove, it just spread the dirt. She and her friends had lots of fun cleaning the kitchen together. Kazuko and Miyoko treated Mei like a queen, which put her in quite a good mood.

August twenty-first. Get up early and water Totoro's seedlings. Do a little weeding. Today's cleaning: toilet and bath. Satsuki and Mei were getting more and more excited. "Mommy's going to take a bath with us." "We can sleep with her all night." They ended the day by having a fight.

"You're seven years older than Mei. You should know better," Tatsuo scolded her.

August twenty-second. Satsuki broke two cups and a plate as she carried the dishes into the living room. She chased Mei into Mommy's room to keep her away from the broken china, and set her to work making a welcome garland out of a paper chain. Mei worked hard to make paper links with scissors and glue.

August twenty-third. Three days till Yasuko came home. Satsuki got Tatsuo to help her air the futons. Next on the list: wash the sheets. Satsuki decided it would be faster to use a bristle brush and scrub the sheets on the washing board. The result: ripped sheets. So much for that idea. In the evening, she was so tired that she lay down for a nap before taking her bath and ended up sleeping till the next morning. Tatsuo had to carry her to bed.

August twenty-fourth. Miyoko and Kazuko dropped by again to help. They cleaned the sliding glass doors that looked out on the garden and hung the welcome garland over the door to Mommy's room. Mei's paper chain wasn't nearly long enough, so Miyoko and Kazuko worked with her to make more. Yasuko would be home in two days.

Satsuki decided to make a welcome sign to hang on the wall. She ground black ink on Tatsuo's inkstone and wrote "Welcome home! Congratulations on your recovery" with a calligraphy brush on a large sheet of paper. As she wrote the characters, she pictured her mother's graceful figure.

Yasuko would cross the footbridge and walk quickly up the path. She would smile. Her cheeks would dimple and her small, white teeth would sparkle. She was always playful, always laughing.

When Mommy saw her room, how happy she'd be!

August twenty-fifth, Friday. One day left. White thunderheads rose against a deep blue sky. The weather was perfect.

Since today was Tatsuo's day to go to the research institute, Granny took charge of Satsuki and Mei. The three of them decided to spend the afternoon in her vegetable garden, collecting fresh vegetables for Yasuko to eat.

Granny's garden was in a clearing on the hill behind her house. It supplied the Ogaki family with all of its vegetables—corn and tomatoes, eggplant and cucumbers, kidney beans and soybeans. The summer vegetables stood in neat rows, with pretty beds of winter cherry and moss rose around the edges of the garden. There were amazingly tall sunflowers in groups of two or three. The garden reminded the children of Granny herself. Now and then a red and blue weathervane would clatter into motion and swivel toward a gust of wind, then fall silent again.

With Granny's help, Satsuki and Mei picked lots of different vegetables. As she walked the rows of plants, the old woman skillfully plucked vegetables and put them in her basket. It was not that easy for Satsuki and Mei. The cucumbers and eggplants pricked their fingers when they tried to pull them off. They couldn't seem to pick the kidney beans at all, no matter how much they tugged. The corn was a mystery; they couldn't tell which ears were ready to harvest and which were not.

Satsuki rushed from plant to plant, exclaiming "Ouch!" and "That itches!" Granny thought she had never seen her so happy. Satsuki had always seemed energetic and cheerful, and it was only now that Granny understood that most of the time, Satsuki was putting up a brave front. Compared to Satsuki, little Mei was her usual self, changeable as the weather, but not feeling things so deeply as her sister.

"How long will your mother be visiting?" Granny asked Satsuki.

"She's going back on Monday. Three days and two nights." Satsuki smiled happily. "But the doctor says that if she does all right, she can come home for good."

"Well, we'd better make sure she eats lots of delicious food while she's here, so she can build up her strength. I'll cook up some red rice to welcome her."

The sun beat down on the garden. It was stiflingly hot. As they sat in the shade of an oak tree and had a snack, Mommy's visit was all the girls could talk about. Even as she ate, Mei wouldn't let go of the big ear of corn she had picked herself.

"Granny, I get to sleep in Mommy's futon tomorrow, when it's nighttime," she said. She took a big bite out of a cucumber they had cooled in the spring that bubbled up near the garden. "Isn't that nice?"

"That should be wonderful," Granny said.

"You can stay at our house too, if you want to," Mei added generously. She put her ear of corn on her shoulder and beamed. She looked so pleased, Granny couldn't resist teasing her a little.

"Mei, did you pick that corn for me? That was very nice of you."

"No! This isn't for you." Mei's eyes widened in surprise. "This is for Mommy. It's not for you."

Satsuki had already eaten a cucumber, a tomato and then another cucumber. "Everything tastes so fresh," she said.

"Telegram! It's a telegram!" Kanta came running up the path between the tomato and taro plants. Satsuki, Mei, and Granny were still smiling when he held the telegram out to Satsuki. "They gave it to Mom. You weren't home," Kanta said in his usual gruff manner.

Satsuki stood up in surprise. "A telegram? For me?" She took the envelope and searched for the addressee. "It says it's for Tatsuo Kusakabe. Daddy won't be home till tonight. Granny, what should I do?"

"Open it. It might be an emergency," Granny said.

Satsuki was nervous. Telegrams usually meant something unpleasant.

She unfolded the telegram. "It says, 'Please contact Shichikokuyama Hospital.' Something must've happened to Mommy!"

Mei clutched her ear of corn tightly and peered anxiously from one face to another. Satsuki looked ready to cry. Kanta looked serious. Granny's face was pale.

"Did Mommy die?" Mei said.

Granny was shocked. "Nonsense. Don't say that, Mei. Satsuki, you'd better telephone right away."

"Phone who? Where?" Satsuki said.

"Why, your father, of course. You know the number, don't you?"

"Yes, at the research institute. But our house doesn't have a phone."

"Kanta, take Satsuki to Uncle's house. She can

use their phone," Granny said. Her tone was stern. This was no time for childish objections, like not wanting to set foot in Uncle's house without a grown-up, or not wanting the rest of the village to see him walking with Satsuki.

Uncle's house was the Ogaki family seat and the largest house in the village. It stood near the zelkovas of Fox Grove. The property was big enough for its own small forest. The house was surrounded by an imposing hedge of holly olive. Kanta only went there two or three times a year, in summer and at New Year's. His parents always acted humble and eager to please Uncle. It made Kanta uncomfortable.

His heart was pounding as he stepped over the broad threshold of Uncle's house into the cool, dark entryway with Satsuki. He took off his cap.

"Hello. It's me, Kanta. Can we use your telephone?"

Satsuki was so distracted with worry that she didn't notice someone getting up from the hearth in the big front room. It was Uncle, Granny's older brother.

"Kanta. What is it?" Uncle stood there on the dark, polished floor looking down at him intently.

"Please let my friend use the telephone. She got

a telegram. Granny said she should call her dad."

Uncle looked impassively at Satsuki. She took a step forward. "Please let me use your telephone. I'm Satsuki Kusakabe."

"Ah." Uncle nodded. "The archaeologist's daughter."

Satsuki said, "Thank you," slipped off her sandals, and went straight to the telephone, which was attached to a pillar at the back of the room. She called the operator, read the number off the wall next to the phone, and gave her Tatsuo's number at the research institute.

Satsuki hung up and sat down on the stool by the pillar to wait for her father to call back. She didn't say a word. She just stared at the floor and tried to keep from crying.

"Is someone ill?" Uncle asked.

"Yes. My mother." That was all Satsuki said.

Uncle was the only person in the village who had been to university. He owned a lot of land and had a hand in most village business. Kanta hardly ever spoke with him. He could never figure out what Uncle was thinking.

Kanta twisted his cap in his hands and stood frozen on the smooth floor of the entryway, watching nervously as Uncle gazed calmly at

Satsuki. Kanta hoped she wouldn't do anything to embarrass him.

When Tatsuo called back, Satsuki told him about the telegram. He told her to wait while he called the hospital. When he called back the second time, Uncle and Kanta knew that Yasuko's visit had been canceled.

"Thank you," Satsuki said weakly as she slipped on her sandals and walked slowly outside. Kanta didn't know what to do. Uncle just motioned with his chin for Kanta to follow her.

When Satsuki realized Kanta was behind her, she ran all the way home, dashing across the footbridge and up the path. As she rushed in from the garden, Mei hurried out of the kitchen looking worried.

When Satsuki saw the paper garland over the door to Mommy's room, the pain struck hard.

She stalked into the room. Her hands were cold and her lips were trembling. She was wrapped in a yellow fog. In a fury, she ripped the welcome sign to shreds. She tore down the garland and the other decorations.

"No no, stop it!" Mei wailed. "That's for Mommy!"

Granny was in the kitchen making rice, but

when she heard Mei's voice she came rushing in. Mei was following Satsuki around the room, whimpering pitifully as her sister destroyed the decorations they had worked so hard to make.

"Quit whining!" Satsuki turned on her and yelled. "She's not coming home. We wasted our time."

"No. Mommy will come." Mei was wide-eyed with fear. "She's coming tomorrow."

"No she isn't, Mei. She's not coming at all. Daddy called the hospital. You don't know anything." Satsuki didn't want to bully her sister, but right now she had to bully someone. "She's sick, you know? So tough luck. If she comes home, she might get even worse."

Mei began to sob miserably. "No, no, no, no!" She shook her head. "I want Mommy. She's coming tomorrow. She promised!"

"You don't care if she dies, do you? All you ever think about is yourself. Fine, do what you want. Just leave me out of it."

Kanta watched helplessly from the garden. Satsuki stood staring at the wall. Granny gently stroked her back.

"Now, Satsuki. There's a good girl. This isn't like you. Please be careful, you're going to scare me."

The moment Granny said this, Satsuki—cheerful, brave Satsuki—began to cry, a loud wail that came from deep inside. She sounded so full of despair that Kanta almost felt like crying too.

Mei stopped crying and stared at her sister in astonishment. Granny put her arms around Satsuki. "Come now, don't worry. I'm sure your mother is all right. Remember what your father said? She'll be just fine."

Satsuki only cried harder. When her mother fell ill, Tatsuo had also said everything was all right and she would be just fine. She'll only be in the hospital for a few days, he'd said, and then the doctor told them that Mommy would've died without medicine.

The tears poured out of Satsuki like a flood.

"Satsuki, if you keep crying like that, the crows and the dragonflies will come from all over Matsugo to see what's wrong. The mountains and the fields will laugh at you." Granny kept talking slowly, soothingly. "No mother would die and leave a sweet little girl like you alone in the world. Everything's going to be just fine, you'll see."

Satsuki cried and cried, enough to call all the crows and all the dragonflies from the mountains and the fields. No one could have guessed that losing her mother's visit would hurt her so much.

It was late afternoon when they noticed that Mei had disappeared. The towering summer clouds were turning blood red and it was getting dark in the house. The shadows in the garden were lengthening.

Satsuki had finally calmed down. She finished filling the bath and went into the living room where Granny was folding clothes. "What's Mei up to?" she asked.

"I don't know," Granny said. "I thought she was with you."

"No. I thought she was with you!"

The evening cicadas were singing loudly in the bamboo grove behind the house. Mei's sandals were nowhere to be found.

"Mei! Mei!" Satsuki called from the back door. The yard was silent and deserted. "Mei, answer me! Mei!"

She ran to the garden. The red of the western sky was deepening. She ran back to the house. Granny was on the veranda, looking uneasily at the sky.

"Did you find her?" Granny said.

"She's not in the garden. Did you look in the house?"

"I looked everywhere. Maybe she went to the bus stop?"

"I don't know. I'll find out!" Satsuki turned to go. Granny put a hand on her shoulder.

"Satsuki, you have to stay calm. Think. Where would Mei go by herself? A place she would go without telling anyone."

Satsuki gasped. She looked stricken. "She might've gone to the hospital!"

"Shichikokuyama? Don't be silly. That's a three-hour walk, even for a grown-up."

"But I have a feeling that's where she went. I'd better try to find her."

Satsuki dashed toward the road with Granny calling after her. On the way she ran right past Kanta, who was coming up the path with a basket of food from his mother.

"Kanta! Leave that here and go get your father, quick as you can," Granny said. "We can't find Mei."

Satsuki cut between the paddies and ran as fast as she could down the narrow dirt road toward the hospital. "Mei! Mei!" she called.

Soon her voice was getting hoarse, but she kept

calling. She couldn't stop running. Soon it would be dark.

"Meeeiii!"

Mei was missing, and it was Satsuki's fault. She had yelled at Mei and told her she didn't care. She had vented all of her frustration on her little sister.

"Mei!"

Satsuki stood on the bridge over the Matsui River and looked fearfully down into the water.

"Mei!"

A farmer was cutting grass at the top of a rise on the other side of the river. Satsuki ran toward him, wiping tears from her eyes. Maybe he had seen Mei. She prayed that he had.

"Please, can you help me?" she called to the farmer anxiously. "Did you see a little girl come by? She's about this big." Satsuki held her hand out to show the farmer.

"A little girl, was it?" the farmer said, looking down at her.

"My sister. She's four."

"I've been here all day, but I can't say I saw a little girl," the farmer said regretfully. The setting sun tinted the grassy slope. Satsuki ran to the top of the rise and looked across the fields and down the road toward the hospital. The road ran through potato fields that spread on either side. The landscape was empty.

"Are you sure she came this way?" the farmer asked. "Better hurry. It'll be dark soon."

The farmer was right. The crows called to each other as they flew to their roosts in the woods. It was already night among the trees. The sun was almost hidden in the dark clouds low in the western sky.

Satsuki looked anxiously toward Shichikokuyama. She hurried down to the road through the tall grass and brambles and kept on running.

"Mei, Mei! Where are you? Somebody help me!"

Had she lost her sister? Satsuki could feel herself starting to cry. The huge clouds over her head were edged with black. The red sky was deepening to darkness.

*Your fault. Your fault. Your fault.*

A three-wheeled motorbike came putting toward her. Satsuki stood in the middle of the road and waved her arms for the driver to stop. The motorbike was coming from Shichikokuyama, but the young couple on the bike just shook their heads and told Satsuki they hadn't seen anyone.

The sound of the idling motor reminded Satsuki

of the day they had moved to the haunted house. She and Mei had ridden in the back of the truck with the books and furniture. How she wished she could turn back the clock to that day!

"Where are you coming from?" asked the man.

"Matsugo," Satsuki told him.

"Matsugo! That's a long way. Well, there's no one up this road, I'm sure of that."

There was no use going further. Mei couldn't have come this far by herself. Satsuki dipped her head in thanks and the young couple drove away.

Satsuki was trudging back when she heard Kanta's voice. She ran toward the sound. Maybe they'd found Mei.

"Satsuki! Satsuki!"

Kanta came down the road on a bicycle that was too big for him. He stood on one pedal and pushed himself along with the other foot.

"Go back to Matsugo," he said. "They haven't found Mei yet."

"But she's not in Matsugo. I'm sure she tried to go to the hospital and got lost somewhere."

*That's right. And it's your fault. You frightened her. You rejected her. You abandoned her.*

"They found a sandal in Shin Pond. Granny's waiting for you."

"The pond? Did Mei drown?"

Mei couldn't swim. Satsuki could see Mei struggling in the dark water, gulping it in. Suffering. Drowning!

*Help me, Satsuki. Please, Mommy. Help me, somebody help me!*

The sea of rice stalks in the paddies was dark and silent as Satsuki ran toward the pond. The paddies gave off a sweet fragrance in the failing light. Satsuki tripped and fell. Irritated, she took off her sandals and ran the rest of the way in her bare feet.

When the pond came into sight, she could see that half the village was watching the search for Mei's body. The village policeman stood by his bicycle. Kanta's father was probing the water with a bamboo pole. Members of the local fire brigade were diving under the water to search the bottom.

"Granny! She's here!" Kazuko pointed to Satsuki running toward them.

*I'm sorry, Mei, help me, Daddy, I'm sorry, Mother, help me.*

Granny went to meet her. The crowd parted. Satsuki ran up to her and Granny held out a little white sandal.

"It's not Mei's!" Satsuki sank to the ground,

gasping for breath. "Her sandals aren't white, they're brown."

Granny fell to her knees too, in relief. Satsuki was still gasping for breath. She felt faint, and for a long time she couldn't stand up. But Mei hadn't drowned. At least that was good news.

## 10. Thank You, Totoro

Satsuki still couldn't catch her breath. She felt sick and her head was spinning. Everything had gone terribly wrong. Where in the world was Mei?

"Looks like you jumped the gun, Granny," Kanta's father said.

"I'm glad I was wrong. I was sure that sandal was Mei's," Granny said.

"All right, everybody, let's search somewhere else," Kanta's father shouted to the men around the pond.

"Listen up, it was a mistake!"

"What?"

"She says it's the wrong sandal!"

The crowd began to break up. The fire brigade members splashed out of the pond. The village policeman told the onlookers to go home. Everyone was talking at the same time.

Satsuki wanted to stand up. She had to find

Mei, right now. The soles of her feet ached. Her knees were skinned and bleeding. Her hands had been cut and stabbed by thorns and sharp grass. Perspiration dripped off her chin into the dust.

Where should she look now? Her breathing was hoarse and ragged. The din that surrounded her died away. Her head was buzzing. When she looked up at Granny, a dark curtain seemed to come down over her vision.

She forced herself to look around. Her face was smeared with perspiration and dust. A shrill clamor erupted from somewhere overhead. Black specks floated in her vision. She squeezed her eyes shut, opened them, and looked up.

The laurel tree glittered in the dying light. There was no wind, but its branches were in constant motion.

Birds. Thousands of birds were coming home to roost in Tsukamori Woods. The laurel was filled with the beating and flapping of tiny wings down to the smallest branch, with thousands of voices chirping and peeping and chattering at the same time.

*They must know where Mei is right now*, Satsuki thought. But she couldn't understand the language of the birds. She was helpless.

She struggled unsteadily to her feet. Her legs were numb, but she forced them to walk away from the pond.

"Satsuki, where are you going?" Granny called after her. "Don't you go missing too. Leave this to Kanta's father and the fire brigade. Take a rest. I'm sure they'll find Mei."

"I'm going home, Granny. There's something I have to do."

*I've got to find Totoro. He must be where Mei said, in the laurel. I'm sure he knows where she is. I know we can't meet him whenever we want. Totoro isn't in the woods just for us. But if I search with all my heart and beg him to help, I know he will. I don't know why I know. I just do.*

A few grown-ups and children remained by the pond. They watched as Satsuki trudged tiredly past. She looked up at the laurel with longing and hope. She couldn't wait to find Totoro.

She walked out of sight of the crowd, jumped across the stream, and climbed straight up the embankment to the cranberry thicket at the edge of the woods. She ran to the spot where Tatsuo had spotted Mei's straw hat the first time she went missing. The foliage was thicker now, and the leaves were a darker green.

Satsuki cautiously parted the branches and peered inside.

"I've got to find Totoro. Please help. It's an emergency. Please let me find him."

The wind whispered in the leaves. The thicket seemed lonely and empty. Satsuki had a feeling that her appeal had gone unheard. Even the birds had fallen silent. The empty windows of the haunted house stared at her wordlessly, as if mocking this girl who had driven her sister away.

Satsuki lifted the tangle of long, slender branches and dived into the tunnel. Mei had insisted over and over that it had taken her straight to Totoro.

"Please take me to Totoro!" Satsuki called in a loud voice.

The tunnel had shown the way to Totoro only once. After that, it had always refused to let Satsuki and Mei visit him. Always, it had sent them packing back to the garden.

It was dark in the tunnel. Branches blocked the way and roots reared up from the ground to catch the unwary. Satsuki crouched over and crept forward awkwardly, shoving branches aside and avoiding the obstacles she could see.

The roots seemed to clutch at her feet. Her foot caught and she toppled forward...

...and felt a soft but powerful push back...

...and she was on her feet again. She stood up straight. The roof of the tunnel was higher than her head. The tunnel seemed to have widened as well. A cool breeze struck her face. The path was thick with soft, spongy moss.

Satsuki ran. The tunnel twisted and weaved through dark foliage. Soot sprites, like inky dandelion fluff, scattered from the moss with each step.

The tunnel twisted and turned, rose and fell. At last she saw a faint, orange light. She ran toward it. As she got closer, she could see it was the entrance to a smaller tunnel.

As she bounded toward the light, her foot caught on a tree root. She plunged headfirst down the hole.

Satsuki tried to break her fall, but there was nothing to hold on to. She wanted to cry out in terror, but her voice caught in her throat. As she rolled and fell, the air seemed to get warmer and thicker.

She landed on something soft. It was too dark to see. She rolled head over heels two or three times and finally stopped. The impact knocked the wind out of her. Her face and outstretched arms came to rest on the ground. It felt furry and warm. A slow, regular sound rose from somewhere beneath her, a muffled pulse like the wings of a great bird rubbing against each other.

As she crawled about, trying to feel her way, she realized she was on a large mound of some sort. The mound was moving up and down in time with the muffled sound.

As she groped in the dark, her hand fell on a stiff, thick wire. She gave it a tug. It tugged back! Just beyond the wire, two huge eyes opened in the dark. Light seemed to come from them.

Satsuki looked into those eyes. They reflected a pale green light. A band of pale green divided each eye. The eyes were beautiful. It was Totoro! Those were Totoro's eyes! Now she noticed his scent too—that sharp smell of dried grass. The muffled sound was Totoro's peaceful breathing.

Totoro's eyes dimmed and began to close slowly. He was falling asleep again. Remembering why she had come, Satsuki grabbed his silky fur and tugged desperately.

"Please wake up. You've got to wake up. Don't go to sleep!" Totoro's eyes opened wider, but only a little.

"Totoro, please help me. We can't find Mei. We

can't find her anywhere. It's my fault. I don't know what to do. I even went toward Shichikokuyama, but I couldn't find her. Please, wake up."

Satsuki felt a wave of despair. She began to sob. Her courage, her determination, everything was just a front. The sadness and helplessness came flooding back. She didn't notice Totoro's long claws closing gently around her.

He held her close and roared. She felt a tremendous power, and everything around her blurred. A rush of air buffeted her and blew through her hair. Twigs and leaves brushed her cheeks as they flew upward.

Totoro's grip loosened. Satsuki opened her eyes and found herself high above the ground. She could see the pond far below. Totoro had lifted her above the tall trees of Tsukamori Woods, all the way to the top of the giant laurel, a hundred feet above the ground. It was like being in a castle. The sun had already set. The sky above the horizon was crimson.

Soon that light would fail. Matsugo would be in darkness.

Satsuki wanted to tell Totoro about the search for Mei. From the top of the laurel she could see everything clearly, even as far as Shichikokuyama.

"See there? Just before the bridge. That's the policeman with his white bicycle. And over there, that old lady is Kazuko's grandmother. But she's going the wrong way. I don't think Mei would've gone toward the school. It's not the same direction as the hospital at all."

Totoro stood silent and motionless in the crimson light. His eyes glowed, but the world he saw was not one Satsuki could see. He held her firmly in his huge paw, turned toward Mount Haké, and gave a long, thunderous roar. At that mighty voice, louder than a hundred steam whistles, the birds rose from the trees in their thousands and flew away as fast as their wings could carry them.

Far to the southwest something was coming quickly through the dark forest, shaking the treetops. A piercing, flutelike call split the sky again and again. The whirlwind burst from the woods and swept across the paddies, leaving a wake of waving rice stalks. It sent the scarecrow's cap flying and came straight toward them, faster and faster, moaning and booming, a solid fist of wind.

The whirlwind threw itself against the base of the laurel and rose toward them. The huge tree swayed and groaned, as if the wind were tugging at its very roots. Then suddenly, the air was calm again.

Before Satsuki's astonished eyes, there on the crown of the laurel stood the cat bus, breathing hard, nostrils flared. Its headlight eyes peered questioningly at Totoro.

Totoro's ears twitched. The cat stared straight ahead and crouched, ready to leap forward. One of its windows widened into a door. Totoro released Satsuki from his paw.

He stood against the dark gray sky and gazed out at the dimming horizon. His eyes were not on Satsuki, but little by little, his long, stiff whiskers pointed upward. He was smiling.

Satsuki climbed into the bus, just as Totoro had on that rainy day when they waited at the bus stop for Tatsuo. The door shrank and became a window again.

A groaning vortex of wind swirled around the cat and tossed the branches of the laurel. Satsuki hardly had time to sit down before the cat sprang into the air. It plunged downward and skimmed the roof of the haunted house, then turned southwest and raced over the paddy fields.

The bus was all cat, inside and out. There were no screws or hinges, no schedule posted inside, no glass in the windows. The floor, ceiling, and seats were covered with glossy fur. There was nothing hard to bump against.

They flew over the paddies with incredible speed. Trees parted like grass as they sped straight through a wood. They flew along the railroad and left a train far behind. As the cat leaped over obstacles and weaved back and forth, its fur held Satsuki in a gentle, mysterious embrace.

They turned sharply, sped along above the surface of the river, turned again, and followed the edge of a dark wood. There, next to a road along the river, stood a row of Jizo statues.

"There she is! We found her!"

Satsuki could see Mei's tiny silhouette, sitting quietly and alone by the statues. She held her ear of corn on her lap.

"Mei! Mei!"

Mei jumped to her feet and began looking this way and that. Satsuki thought the cat would stop, but as soon as she called to her sister, it leaped into the sky over the woods and left Mei behind.

"Mei, stay there! Don't move!"

The cat plunged earthward like a comet, trailing points of light. It skimmed across fields of plume grass, bounded over pine groves, and carried

Satsuki to Shichikokuyama Hospital. It rounded
the tall pine that stood outside Yasuko's window
and sped off like a whirlwind toward Matsugo.

But for just a moment, Satsuki caught a glimpse
of her mother's smile.


"I've got to help Mei!"

Satsuki wanted to run, but something was
wrong. She opened her eyes and found herself lying facedown in the dark. She was in the tunnel in
the cranberry thicket.

"Satsuki! Satsuki!" She heard voices. Was
someone looking for her?

She lifted her head and realized she was just
inside the tunnel entrance. She was exhausted,
but managed to crawl through the foliage into the
open air.

"There she is! Granny, over here!" It was Kanta.
Granny hurried over. Two men and a woman fol-
lowed her. They had to be from the village, but
Satsuki didn't recognize them. Kanta's little brother
Shigeta was there, and Miyoko.

"There you are! We were worried sick."
Granny looked relieved. "You said you were going
home, but you looked so worn out, I thought I

better look after you. But there was no one in the house."

The old woman from the village peered kindly at Satsuki. She was dressed for work in the fields. A shirtless young man stood next to her. Satsuki had seen him earlier, diving in the pond.

"What were you doing in there?" the man from the fire brigade said.

"Spirited away," the old woman said. She turned to look curiously at the house. "Haunted. I always said so."

Satsuki clutched Granny's arm and struggled to her feet. "Four or five Jizo statues. Next to the road, near some trees. That's where she is. We have to go right now."

"Near trees? You mean the Jizos at Kobinata?" Granny said, mystified.

"Yes. I looked down and saw Mei there."

"You mean you went there? You saw her yourself?" the third villager asked. He was an old farmer with a broad, bent back.

"Yes. Yes, I saw her."

"But...how?"

Kanta, Miyoko, and Shigeta stared wide-eyed with surprise.

"I have to go," Satsuki said. "It's getting dark. We don't have much time." She was anxious to get moving. She knew no one would believe her story anyway.

"Now you listen to me, young lady." Granny took her arm. "I won't hear of it. You're on your last legs already. Kanta, get yourself over there on the bicycle and be quick about it. Find Mei and keep her there till we come. We'll bring Satsuki straightaway."

"I'll take her," the young man from the fire brigade said as he watched Kanta sprinting away. He slipped a t-shirt over his head. "I've got a bicycle with a trailer down the road. She can ride in that."

The old woman spoke quietly to the farmer with the bent back. "Do you think the child's really there? There's something odd about this." The man just scratched his gray head.

As Granny, Satsuki, and the young man started walking toward the road, Granny looked over her shoulder. "She's there. This girl knows what she's talking about. I think she had some special help. Now we'd better hurry," she said to Satsuki, who just smiled and nodded.

The man stood on the pedals and went as fast as he could. Satsuki and Granny sat on the trailer bed. Pebbles scattered as they sped along. Miyoko and Shigeta trailed behind, running as fast as they could.

Before the river, they turned onto a road that ran between the paddies and headed straight down it until the road curved around a stand of trees.

"We're over here! Come on!"

Through the evening mist they could make out six upright shapes, just off the road. The voice was Kanta's. For once he sounded truly happy. "Mei's here! She's fine!"

All the way, Granny's face had been grim and serious. Now she sighed with relief. "Praise heaven," she said quietly.

Satsuki leaped from the trailer and ran to her sister. "Mei, I was so worried! I didn't know what to do." She gave Mei a hug.

Miyoko and Shigeta soon caught up. Everyone was laughing with relief. Mei stood in the center, looking happy and a little embarrassed.

"I wanted to go to the hospital," she began, very

earnestly. "But I got lost in the trees. Everywhere was trees. I was lost, so I came back."

Mei looked awkwardly at Satsuki. "And, and, it was really far. I got tired, so I took a rest here."

"Better tell everyone in the village we found her," Granny said to the young man. He nodded, got on his bicycle and pedaled off.

Granny and the children turned for home. The evening breeze blew gently and swayed the heavy stalks of the rice in the paddies. The children straggled along, spread out over the road.

"I'm sorry I yelled at you, Mei," Satsuki said.

"It's okay." Mei smiled. "I'm not mad. I'm a good girl."

"It's true, you really are. You didn't even cry."

"Not like someone I know," Granny said with a chuckle.

"I hardly ever cry now," Shigeta said. He looked indignant.

Kanta pushed the bicycle along with one foot on the pedal. "You know what? When I found Mei, she was playing with the statues."

"Playing?" Satsuki couldn't believe her ears.

"Yeah," Kanta said. "Right, Mei?"

Mei nodded. "I was feeding them."

"You know what she was doing?" Kanta said.

"She was mixing grass and stuff with the flowers people left and putting it in front of the statues."

"Isn't that bad luck?" Miyoko said to Granny, a bit frightened.

Granny laughed. "Don't worry. Even statues need a bite to eat every now and then."

"You were actually playing?" Satsuki rolled her eyes. She had been so worried! "I'm surprised you weren't scared."

"I wasn't lost!" Mei almost shouted. "I was going home. But the cat bus came and you told me not to move. I did what you said." She puffed out her chest proudly. "I was playing 'cause I had to wait. That's why!"

It wasn't until Matsugo was wrapped in darkness that Tatsuo finally returned from Shichikokuyama Hospital.

"I'm glad to see you two looking so cheerful," said Tatsuo to Satsuki and Mei, somewhat surprised. "I was afraid you'd be awfully disappointed about Mommy." The girls beamed at him.

"I have some good news. Mommy's leaving the hospital around the middle of September, and she doesn't have to go back. She just has a cold now. I think she got a little overexcited about coming home."

Tatsuo had no idea of all the amazing things his daughters were waiting to tell him. "It's been hard for Mommy, being separated from us for so long," he said. "But it won't be long now. I hope you can wait just a little longer."

*What an exhausting day!* Satsuki thought. And she sprawled out on the tatami and fell fast asleep.

Matsugo was a small village, and it didn't take Tatsuo long to visit everyone who helped search for his daughter. Rumor had it that she had been spirited away by a supernatural being.

The evening they found Mei, Satsuki developed a fever and had to spend the weekend in bed, but soon she was back to her cheerful, adventurous self.

When the sisters visited the Tsukamori laurel to give thanks, a sudden gust of wind seemed to wave the branches in reply.

So many things in life pass quickly. Why did it take so long for the middle of September to arrive?

*Just like we can't see Totoro whenever we want,* thought Satsuki as she played with her friends, *the really important things feel like they'll never come.* She shook her head.

Still, after August is over, September must follow. And the days must pass, one at a time.

When the day they had been longing for finally came, Yasuko crossed the bridge and walked up the path toward Mei and Satsuki. Her face was shining. When she saw the house, she laughed with joy.

"Oh, dear! Just look at this place. It's falling apart!"

## About the Authors

Hayao Miyazaki is one of Japan's most beloved animation directors. His first feature, *The Castle of Cagliostro*, was released in 1979. His film *Nausicaä of the Valley of the Wind*, based on his own manga, was released in 1984. In 1985 Miyazaki cofounded Studio Ghibli, through which he directed the box-office smashes *Princess Mononoke* (1997) and *Spirited Away* (2001), which won the Golden Bear at the 2002 Berlin International Film Festival and the Academy Award® for Best Animated Feature Film in 2003. *Howl's Moving Castle* (2004) received the Osella Award for technical achievement at the 2004 Venice International Film Festival. In 2005 VIFF awarded Miyazaki the Golden Lion Award for Lifetime Achievement. His other acclaimed films include *My Neighbor Totoro*, *Kiki's Delivery Service*, and *Ponyo*. Miyazaki's essays, interviews, and memoirs have been collected in *Starting Point: 1979–1996* and *Turning Point: 1997–2008*. His final film, *The Wind Rises*, was nominated for both a Golden Globe and Academy Award®.

Tsugiko Kubo was born in Kanagawa, Japan. After an acting career with the Mingei Theater Company, Kubo started writing children's books. Her books include *July 6th, Sunny Then Quarrel, Haruka-chan's Haruka Day*, and *You Would Not Have Forgotten*.

*Also Available!*

# My Neighbor
# TOTORO
## Picture Book

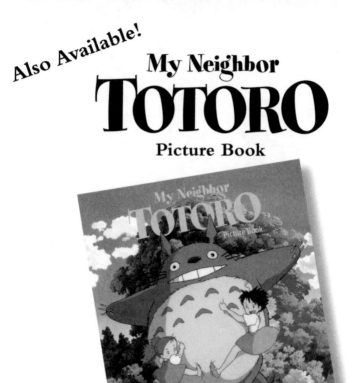

Written & directed by
## HAYAO MIYAZAKI

Experience Hayao Miyazaki's classic film *My Neighbor Totoro* in a whole new way.

The *My Neighbor Totoro Picture Book* tells the story of Mei, Satsuki, and their new magical friends with easy-to-read text, pictures from the actual film, maps, character guides, and more. This oversized art-style book is fun for the whole family!

$19.99 USA/$22.99 CAN/£12.99 UK  ISBN: 978-1-4215-6122-6

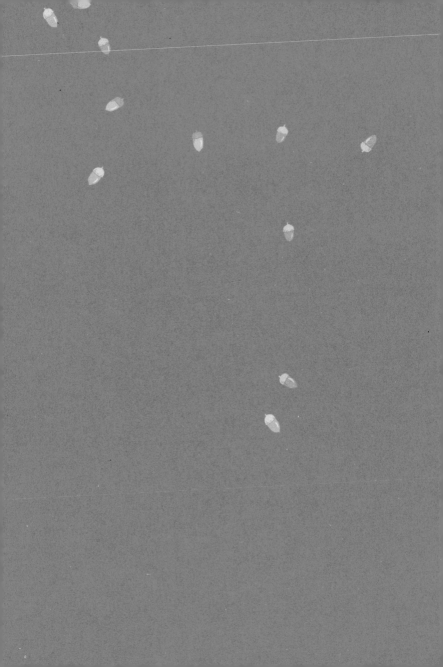